The Engineer of Evil

Adventures in Reason

Kris Langman

Post Hoc Publishing

The Engineer of Evil
Copyright © 2021 by Kris Langman
Print Edition
Post Hoc Publishing

Chapter One

❖

A Royal Mess

"NO, NOT GREY satin," Gwen hissed through the tarp at the back of the used-clothing stall. "Mother hates me in grey satin. She says I look like a grumpy rain cloud sent to ruin her dinner parties."

Fuzz sighed loudly and resumed rummaging through the pile of dresses. Nikki put her eye to a hole in the tarp and watched Fuzz drag a red velvet gown out of the pile. He held it up and shook it. A cloud of dust billowed off it and he choked back a cough.

Gwen shook her head vigorously even though Fuzz couldn't see her through the tarp. "Red velvet is for ladies with bad reputations. Mother would faint dead away if she saw me in that. Why don't I just come out there and pick a dress myself?"

Fuzz frantically waved at the tarp, shaking his head. "No! The stall owner is right over there. She's sitting on a bench eating a pork pie and keeping a beady eye on both of her stalls. She can't see me cause I'm table-height, but she'd spot you immediately. How about this pale blue silk?" He rolled up the dress and shoved it under the bottom of the tarp.

Gwen snatched it up and held it in front of her. "Not bad," she said. "It's got a small tear in one sleeve, but I don't think anyone will notice. Find me a cloak to go with it. A blue one if you can find it."

"This isn't a dressmaker's shop!" hissed Fuzz. "I'm not here to help Madame find a dress for the ball. And besides, the stall owner has finished her pie."

Nikki, Gwen, and Curio heard more rustling noises, then Fuzz suddenly appeared around the corner of the stall carrying a pink satin cloak lined in purple velvet.

"Here," he said, thrusting the cloak at Gwen.

Gwen rolled her eyes as she took it. "Mother's going to have a fit when she sees this. It doesn't go at all with the blue dress and Mother is very particular about clothes."

"Just tell her it's the latest fashion," snapped Fuzz. "Tell her our dear deceased Queen used to wear one just like it. Now come on. Let's get out of here. The Rounders patrol this market every hour and we're pushing our luck."

Fuzz led them along the stalls to an empty shack that was used to store chickens sold at the market. Gwen wrinkled her nose at the smell as she ducked inside to change. She emerged a few minutes later holding the skirt of the blue silk dress out of the mud. Nikki helped her fasten the dress up the back and adjusted the pink cloak.

Fuzz stuffed Gwen's old brown dress into a rucksack he had "borrowed" from a stall. "Okay," he said. "Follow me. Keep your heads down and don't talk to anyone."

Nikki and Curio pulled their page caps down low over their eyes and they all followed Fuzz out of the market and through the back alleys of Cogent Town. After lots of doubling back to check if they were being followed they arrived at a wooden tavern which took up a whole city block. Drunken laughter floated out from its windows. The building had carved gables and wrought-iron columns holding up a wide porch. Baskets of scarlet geraniums hung from the columns. Loud shouts and the clink of glasses could be heard when the front door opened.

"Right," said Fuzz, his sharp eyes searching the cobbled square in front of the tavern for anyone who might be watching them. A few drunks were snoring against the side of the building and a donkey was drinking from a watering trough, but otherwise the square was empty. "This is the Fox and Fig. I've spent many an evening here and the owner knows me. I don't think he'll betray me to the Rounders or the castle guards. This is also the King's nephew's favorite tavern. It shouldn't be hard to convince him to come here. The mansion of the Duchess of Falsa, where he's staying, is just down that street."

"Yes, I know where it is," said Gwen. "What about Athena? Is she already inside the tavern?"

Fuzz shook his head. "Her leg is paining her, so she decided to stay back at our hideout. It's a shame, as Bertie likes her better than me. She used to coddle him when he was a boy and call him ridiculous names like Sweet Little Bumpkins and Bertie the Brilliant. Me he probably remembers mainly for dunking his head into horse troughs when he drank too much. Still, I'm pretty sure he'll meet with me. Though we might have to take him to Athena if he balks at getting involved in our plans. He's not the bravest of princelings."

"Is he really a prince?" asked Nikki. "I thought you said he was the King's nephew, not his son."

"He is," said Fuzz. "But the King and Queen didn't have any children, so Bertie kind of got promoted to unofficial prince."

"Does that mean he's next in line for the throne?" asked Nikki, ideas starting to sprout in her head.

Fuzz gave her a suspicious glance. "Don't make any plans to put Bertie at the head of a rebellion against Rufius. Bertie would faint dead away at the sight of arrows aimed in his direction or any Knights of the Iron Fist charging at him. Our goal is just to convince him to talk to his pals in the nobility. There are some good people among them, believe it or not. Some of them hide behind a mask of frippery and fancy clothes, but don't be fooled. There are some sharp minds surrounding the King, trying to do what's best for the Realm. They've just had to hide their true colors recently as Rufius's power has grown. It won't help anyone if they were to get thrown into the dungeons of Castle Cogent."

"The Prince of Physics is openly defying Rufius down in Kingston," said Nikki. "And he's not in a dungeon."

"The Prince is a special case," said Fuzz. "He has more power in the Realm, especially in the southern parts, then anyone except the King. And the people of Kingston are extremely loyal to him. He helps the poor, props up the local fishing industry, patrols the coastline, and just does a good job in general of governing that part of the Realm and maintaining order. It's a different story up here in the north where our current King is not exactly a beacon of hard work and good governance. His laziness has caused the people to lose trust in him and has allowed twits like Rufius to grab power. Anyway, now is not the time to stand around gabbing about politics. Get yourselves inside the mansion of the Duchess of Falsa and try to convince Bertie to come here."

Fuzz disappeared inside the Fox and Fig.

Gwen motioned Nikki and Curio to get behind her. "Each of you grab a corner of my cloak and hold it out of the dirt," she said. "Keep your heads down and don't talk to anyone if you can help it."

They proceeded awkwardly down the street, Gwen with her head held high and Nikki and Curio trying to hold up the cloak without yanking it off of Gwen's shoulders. The bakers delivering bread, the boys running errands, and the farm women carrying baskets of apples all dodged out of Gwen's way and stared after her as she passed.

"Here we are," said Gwen at last, coming to a halt in front of a three-story mansion built out of white marble. Lilac bushes waved in the breeze under its first-floor windows. Someone was playing a violin inside the house and the melody drifted out into the street. At the top of the steep front stairs two footmen in green velvet livery stared down at them. Gwen gave the footmen a little wave and gracefully ascended the stairs.

"Goodness," she said when she reached the top. "These stairs get steeper every time I climb them. Please be so kind as to inform the Duchess that I am here."

One of the footmen raised an eyebrow. "And who shall I say is calling, Miss?"

Gwen arched an eyebrow in return. "Why the daughter of Lady Ursula, Duchess of Malaprop, of course. I realize that I haven't spent much time in Cogent Town recently, but I didn't realize that I had become a complete unknown. If I'm not careful I'll have to relinquish my title and stoop to selling flowers on the street." She gave an artificial little laugh. "Now, please be a good boy and announce me. I don't care to spend all day standing on the doorstep."

The footman gave her a curt nod and disappeared inside, firmly closing the front door.

Gwen stared serenely at the lilac bushes while Nikki and Curio stared down at the ground. They didn't have long to wait. The front door was flung open and Gwen's mother appeared on the doorstep.

"Gwen, what on earth!" Lady Ursula dropped the tiny pink poodle she was carrying and grabbed Gwen by the arm. She yanked her inside, Nikki and Curio in tow. "I don't hear from you for months and now here you are, popping up at the Duchess's front door with two of the King's pages attached to you."

Gwen gave a dismissive wave in the direction of Curio. "I needed an escort. I didn't want to walk the streets of Cogent Town alone, so the King kindly offered me two of his pages."

"Yes, yes. Very sensible," said Lady Ursula impatiently. "But why are you here? I thought you were in Deceptionville. And you haven't been to see the Duchess since you were ten years old. She very rightly banned you from this house after you dumped that nasty substance in her fireplace. The sparks set her spaniel on fire. The poor little thing had a bald head for a month."

Gwen waved this away. "It was just a pinch of sodium. Completely harmless, and the sparks made such a lovely yellow color."

Lady Ursula snorted. "It wasn't harmless to the spaniel. For years afterward she refused to stay in any room which had a fireplace."

While they were talking Lady Ursula's pink poodle wandered over to Nikki and gave her the stink eye. The poodle started to growl and Nikki wondered if it was the same dog Lady Ursula had been petting when she, Fuzz, and Athena had visited Muddled Manor. Nikki tried to gently nudge the dog away with her foot, which only turned its growl into loud yapping.

"Bitsy!" exclaimed Lady Ursula. "Stop that at once! You'll wake the Duchess from her nap." She snatched up the poodle and tucked it under her arm, where it continued to glare at Nikki. "The Duchess has a dreadful headache, poor thing," said Lady Ursula. "She and the King's nephew were up half the night chatting and drinking sparkling wine. That kind of thing might be fine for a young person like Bertie, but for a refined, mature lady like the Duchess it has unfortunate consequences. You remember Bertie, don't you? You used to play together as children."

"Oh, is Bertie here?" asked Gwen in an innocent voice. "Why, I haven't seen him since I was seven years old. Remember what a naughty boy he was? He used to put frogs in your powdered wigs. How you used to jump when they slid down your nose!"

Lady Ursula gave a dignified sniff and didn't reply.

"I'd love to see Bertie again," continued Gwen. "Where is he?"

"He's in the dining room having a very late breakfast," said Lady Ursula. "I suppose you can see him if you wish, but you still haven't told me what you're doing in Cogent Town. And why you look so unlike your usual drab self. I must say, that shade of pale blue looks very nice with your coloring. It brings out the blue of your eyes. Though that pink cloak was a mistake. It is positively hideous. Why don't we go to the Duchess's dressmaker this afternoon? I'll have her make you a lovely frock. They just got in a batch of silk from the Southern Isles."

"Maybe tomorrow," said Gwen. "I just want to say a quick hello to Bertie and then I have to dash. Some friends are expecting me for tea." She beckoned imperiously for Nikki and Curio to follow her.

They hurried down a long hallway lined with mirrors in gilt frames. Gwen's cloak flashed in them like a streak of pink fire. The dining room they entered at the end of the hall had floor-to-ceiling windows open to the morning breeze. The cream satin tablecloth covering the dining table flapped in the breeze and folded pieces of parchment were being blown hither and thither around the room like paper birds.

"I say," said a young man in a turquoise silk tunic and black leggings. "Help me collect these calling cards, will you?" He made a sudden leap and just managed to catch one of the pieces of parchment before it blew out the window. "They're invitations to dine with just about every noble in Cogent Town. Not that I really plan to dine with them all, but I still have to send my regrets. I promised Uncle that I'd do a better job of observing the social niceties than the last time I was in town."

Gwen grabbed a card as it flew past her nose and Nikki and Curio dropped her cloak and scrambled around the room snatching up the pieces of parchment. They handed them to the young man, who dumped them into an empty soup tureen. Gwen dropped her catch into the tureen and sat down gracefully at the table.

The young man plopped down at the head of the table and eyed her quizzically. "I say, you look awfully familiar. Didn't we meet at one of Lady Hyacinth's card parties? I lost a monstrous amount of gold playing bridge at her house. To a blonde young lady who was winning hand after hand. I think she was cheating, quite frankly. Was that you? My memory of the event is a bit fuzzy. I was, er, under the weather at the time."

Gwen laughed. "No, Bertie. It wasn't me. I haven't seen you since I was seven. You came to Muddled Manor with the King and Queen. You gave our servants a terrible time of it. Remember when you accidentally caught the tablecloth in the buckle of your shoe and an entire feast came crashing to the floor? Our cook nearly quit. Mother had to double her salary."

"Little Gwennie!" exclaimed Bertie. "Oh my golly, it *is* you! Why it's been ever such a long time. And what a lovely young lady you've grown up to be. Tall, too. I believe you're even taller than I am." He reached for the flowered china teapot in front of him. "A spot of tea while we chat about old times? I'll get the Duchess's cook to make some more scones. She puts orange peel in them and they're simply marvelous."

Gwen shook her head. "Not right now, Bertie. There's an old friend of yours at the Fox and Fig who's dying to see you again. Why don't we dash over there? I'm not busy at the moment, and your dinner invitations can wait."

Bertie jumped up at once. "Smashing! Anything to get out of this mausoleum. It's the dullest place in town. I was going to stay in my usual quarters up at the castle, but things are a bit odd up there right now, judging from the rumors I've heard."

"There are bigger problems up there than just rumors," said Gwen, giving him a sharp look. "Don't you know what's been going on in the Realm?"

Bertie gave an apologetic shrug. "Afraid not. I try to stay out of politics. Uncle keeps trying to get me involved but so far I've managed to dodge him. I think he intends to hand over his crown to me eventually, but between you and me I'd rather become a street sweeper. People get all excited by the pomp and glamour of the throne but they don't realize how beastly the actual business of ruling is. People are constantly bringing their petty little problems to you, expecting you to solve them instantly. And besides, I've been out of the country for years. Went way up north to the little river towns past our borders. Lovely country up there. Rushing streams, meadows filled with flowers. Took a few mates with me and we wandered around, staying in local inns, until we settled in one of the larger towns. Place called Friebergen. Spent my days enjoying the company of the local lads, drinking the local ale, and playing cards at the casino. Got messages from the King once in a while, asking me to come back to the Realm, but I was having such a delightful time that I kept postponing my homecoming. I don't think anyone really missed me here anyway."

"Maybe not," said Gwen, "but there's someone who really needs to talk to you. Come on. Let's get over to the Fox and Fig before it gets too late. It should be quiet now, but you know better than anyone that the fights can get out of control later in the day."

"Of course," said Bertie, rising from the table. "We'll go at once. I wouldn't want any drunken louts throwing chairs at your lovely blond head."

Gwen nodded and stood up, motioning to Nikki and Curio to hold up the ends of her cloak again. Bertie gave Gwen his arm and they had nearly made it to the front door when a loud shriek behind them made them freeze in their tracks.

"Your Highness, where are you going?"

They all turned. An elderly lady in a pink silk dressing gown was clutching her throat, her eyes wide. Her fluffy white hair was standing straight up and her yellowish complexion shaded to pale green around her mouth, as if she'd been ill.

"You promised we'd do the rounds of the gaming tables to-day," the elderly woman whined. "I haven't been out of the house in ages and I was so looking forward to showing you off. The Count of Calumnia will be at the card tables this afternoon. He told me so himself. He was so looking forward to a quiet game with you."

Bertie laughed. "He was so looking forward to relieving me of all of my gold, you mean. Don't worry, my dear Duchess. I'm sure I'll have time to escort you to the casino. But right now I'm off for a stroll with little Gwennie."

The Duchess tottered toward them and Nikki quickly pulled her pages's cap low over her eyes. She'd just realized why the elderly lady looked familiar. The Duchess of Falsa had been in the town of Popularnum when she, Athena, and Fuzz had tried to rid the townsfolk of their very expensive habit of wearing huge silk ruffs round their necks. To replace the ruffs Athena had made very clever hair ornaments for the ladies of the town, weaving them out of corn husks which Nikki and Fuzz had painted bright colors. When they'd gathered the ladies of the town together to show them the ornaments the Duchess had been there. Nikki herself had arranged an ornament in the Duchess's fluffy white hair.

"Wait," said the Duchess, her arm outstretched towards Bertie. "I'll accompany you on your walk. It will only take me a moment to change. Let me just summon my maid. I don't know where the girl is hiding. She's never around when I want her." She disappeared down the mirrored hallway, calling for her maid in a loud voice.

"Quick!" said Bertie, opening the front door and shooing them all outside. "Before she comes back! The Duchess is a clingy old girl. She hasn't given me a moment's peace. If her cook wasn't such a master of her craft I'd find another place to spend my nights."

Their progress down the front stairs of the mansion and along the streets of Cogent Town back to the Fox and Fig had the air of a parade about it. Bertie took Gwen's arm and strolled down the middle of the street, with Nikki and Curio bringing up the rear. Farm carts and the carriages of the nobility swerved and came to a full stop to avoid hitting them. Bertie just waved at them as he passed. When a farmer shook his fist at them because his sudden stop had caused a load of pumpkins to smash onto the cobblestones Bertie merely tossed him a gold coin and kept on walking.

When they arrived at the Fox and Fig both Nikki and Gwen breathed a sigh of relief. Gwen still held her head up at a regal angle, but Nikki could tell that having to act the part of a pretentious noblewoman was wearing on her.

Gwen took off her pink cloak and handed it to Nikki. "Take care of this, page. The two of you can wait for me out here."

Nikki nodded and folded the cloak. She and Curio sat down on a bench near the horse troughs as Bertie escorted Gwen into the tavern.

The sun was warm and a sparrow chirped quietly nearby. Nikki was just sinking into a doze when a loud gurgle startled her awake.

"Sorry, Miss," said Curio. "That was just me innards rumbling. I wish Mr. Bertie had offered us a couple of those scones he was on about. They sounded mighty appealing."

Nikki patted him on the shoulder. "Try not to think about the scones. It'll just make you hungrier. And don't worry, Fuzz will scrounge something for us to eat once he's done talking to Bertie. Or done talking to the Prince, I guess I should say. It won't be good if someone should walk by and overhear a page referring to the King's nephew as Bertie."

Curio picked a dandelion out of the grass under the bench and rolled it between his fingers. "Maybe it's not my place to say so, Miss, but this Mr. Bertie doesn't strike me as very prince-like. He seems like what us back in D-ville would call a feather. You know, a lightweight."

Nikki laughed. "Yeah. I got that impression too. But Fuzz and Athena think he can be helpful, and they should know. They're the experts when it comes to Castle Cogent and all its palace intrigues." She tucked a lock of hair back under her page cap and surveyed the sleepy square in front of the Fox and Fig. It was mid-morning, probably a slow time for taverns. A pair of chickens pecked at the grass nearby, and a tired-looking donkey dozed in front of a watering trough.

Curio gave a big yawn and stretched himself out on the grass under the bench. "Might as well get a bit of shut-eye while we're waiting, Miss."

Curio was soon fast asleep and Nikki dozed on the bench, listening to his snores. The soft grass looked extremely inviting, but it seemed like a bad idea for both of them to fall asleep in public. They were protected by their page-uniform disguises, but she still felt like she should keep watch.

Her head was drooping and her eyes closing when the clip-clop of horses' hooves startled her out of her doze. She looked up to see two men on horseback ride into the square. One was a pale, slim man in a dark tunic and sandals. The other was a strongly-built blond man in rough working-man's clothes.

Nikki's mouth dropped open, her whole body frozen in disbelief.

The men dismounted, tied their horses to a hitching post, and went into the tavern without even a glance in her direction.

As the door of the Fox and Fig banged behind them Nikki reached under the bench and frantically shook Curio by the shoulder.

"Ten more minutes," mumbled Curio. "Then I'll feed the pigs."

"Wake up!" hissed Nikki. "It's Rufius and Darius!"

"What's that, Miss?" asked Curio, crawling out from under the bench and rubbing his eyes. "Me ears are still asleep. It sounded like you said Rufius and Darius."

"I did!" said Nikki. "They went into the tavern."

"That don't make no sense, Miss," said Curio. "Darius is in some dungeon somewhere. He was captured last time we saw him. Back in ImpHaven. He was surrounded by armed knights."

"I know," said Nikki. "But he just rode into the square, got off his horse, and walked right past me."

"Was you maybe dreaming, Miss?" asked Curio. "I have the strangest dreams sometimes, specially when I'm hungry. Like right now, before you woke me up, I was dreaming that a giant scone was chasing me through the streets of D-ville cause it wanted to eat me. I kept throwing rocks at it but the rocks turned into raisins and stuck to it."

Nikki shook her head impatiently. "No, I was wide awake. Come on. I don't have any idea why Darius is wandering around free as a bird, but we have to warn Gwen about Rufius. She's not in disguise like us, and if he catches sight of her he'll have her arrested.”

Nikki headed for the front stairs of the Fox and Fig, but Curio caught her arm.

“Not that way, Miss. I don’t know the ways of this old tavern like Mr. Fuzz does, but I’ve been here a few times. There’s a servants entrance around back where they bring in the casks of ale. They’ll be less likely to spot us if we come in that way.”

Chapter Two

Darius

"TAKE YOUR FEATHER off, Miss" whispered Curio. "They'll not be so likely to see you."

"Oh, right," whispered Nikki. She yanked at the yellow feather on top of her page cap until it came off. She and Curio had managed to get into the Fox and Fig without attracting attention. Pages seemed to be a common sight in the tavern. They'd passed several others in their purple uniforms hanging around the back entrance, message bags slung from their shoulders.

They strolled casually into the crowded main room and ducked behind an overturned table pushed up against the back wall. Nearby a huge fireplace belched puffs of black smoke into the room. The remains of a pig smoldered on a spit hung inside the fireplace.

Nikki stifled a cough and cautiously peered over the top of the table. She spotted Rufius at once. He'd installed himself at a table in the center of the room and was delicately sipping some kind of liquor which glowed green in the smoky light. He was surrounded by a large group of men who were all watching him intently. Darius was seated next to Rufius, staring moodily down at the table.

"I don't see Fuzz or Gwen or Bertie," Nikki whispered.

Curio poked his head over the edge of the table. "Hmm. You'd think that pink cloak of Miss Gwen's would stand out like a rose in a pig sty." He scanned the room carefully, then nodded in the direction of a nearby staircase. "They might be in one of the fancy rooms upstairs," he said. "The Fox and Fig don't have guest rooms for sleeping in, but they do have what they call parlors, for rich folks who want privacy while drinking or lunching or playing cards."

Nikki glanced at the staircase. It was only a few feet away and there were lots of people standing around in groups and chatting while they drank their ale. There were plenty of tall people to hide behind. "I think we can go up without Rufius seeing us, but are pages allowed up there?"

"Oh, sure," said Curio. "They take messages up there all the time. Come on, let's go now. Rufius the Ruffian isn't looking this way. He's drinking his glow worm."

"His what?" asked Nikki, thinking she hadn't heard right.

"His glow worm," said Curio, making a face. "That's what the green stuff he's drinking is called. The story is that it's made out of tiny green worms found in caves in the Haunted Hills. They glow green in the darkness of the caves, and when you squish the worms the juice what comes out glows green too."

Nikki felt her stomach turn. "He's drinking squished-worm juice?"

Curio shrugged. "Never quite believed the worm story me self. The educated types back in D-ville used to say it was made from some kind of mineral that glows. Just a tiny amount mixed in with alcohol. Seems like a more believable story to me. They also used to say that drinking too much of it could cause your skin to become really pale and ghost-y like, and that it could drive you insane."

"Huh," said Nikki, peering over the table edge at Rufius's

pale face. Zinc silicate was a fluorescent mineral which could glow green, but she'd never heard of it being used in drinks. The element radium which had been discovered by Madame Curie also glowed, but its glow was more blue than green. It could make you very sick from radiation poisoning, which would make you very pale, but radium was very difficult to get. It was a byproduct of uranium mining, and she very much doubted that there was any uranium mining going on in the Realm. She shrugged and ducked down again. "Come on," she said, motioning to Curio. "Stay low and be quick."

They crawled out from behind the table and scurried as fast as they could to the staircase. A woman in a black silk dress waved at them as they passed and called out something about taking a message up to the castle, but they ignored her and she just shrugged and resumed drinking her glass of ale.

They made it to the stairs and ran up as fast as they could. The second floor landing opened onto a narrow oak-paneled hallway with a dozen closed doors leading off it. A calico cat was sunning itself on the sill of the landing's dusty window, but otherwise the hallway was empty.

"How are we going to find the right room?" whispered Nikki. "We can't knock on each door."

"Follow me, Miss," said Curio. "There's a top floor with only a few rooms. That's where the bigwigs meet. My guess is that the owner of the tavern took one look at Mr. Bertie and Miss Gwen in their fancy clothes and brought them right up to the top floor."

He led Nikki down to the far end of the hallway, to the last closed door. It looked like all the other doors, but when he pushed it open it revealed a narrow staircase winding up to the roof. The well-worn steps made loud creaking noises as they climbed. Nikki winced at each creak, but no one appeared above them to see who was approaching.

At the top was a small landing right under the eaves of the tavern. Three closed doors led off the landing. Curio darted to the first door and put his ear to it. He shook his head and motioned her to the second one. Nikki put her ear to it but heard nothing. When they tried the third door she could hear faint voices. One of them sounded like a woman's voice.

"I can't tell if that's Gwen or not," whispered Nikki. "We don't want to barge in on complete strangers. They might have us arrested or something."

Curio motioned her to the side of the door. "Get back out of sight, Miss. If it's not Miss Gwen, well, nobody'll recognize me. Me face isn't on wanted posters like yours is." He adjusted his page cap and knocked on the door.

Nikki could feel vibrations coming through the wall as heavy footsteps came toward the door. She frowned. Both Gwen and Bertie were tall, but thin and light on their feet. They wouldn't have such a heavy tread. And Fuzz would hardly make any sound at all. She was about to grab Curio away from the door when it opened.

Curio's mouth fell open but no sound came out. His head tilted back as he gawked at someone towering above him. A large hand reached out and grabbed the front of his page jacket, pulling him inside the room.

Nikki made a frantic grab at him and was hauled inside as well. She aimed a kick at the leg of their assailant but he stepped back with a laugh.

"Calm down, Miss. We're all friends here."

Startled, Nikki tilted her head back just as Curio had done and stared into the amused eyes of the Prince of Physics.

"Stop abusing the Prince and come have something to eat," called Fuzz, waving at them from a table by the window.

Gwen and Bertie were seated next to him at a polished table

piled high with rolls, mashed potatoes, a roast turkey and a blueberry pie oozing juice and topped with whipped cream. Curio lost no time in pulling out a chair and grabbing a turkey leg. Nikki followed more slowly, glancing around the room, hoping to find Athena seated in one of the armchairs tucked into the corners.

"Don't worry," said Fuzz. "The Prince has sent someone to collect her. He's having her sent to his house here in Cogent Town. We'll all stay there. It'll be safer and a lot more comfortable than our leaky hideout."

Nikki nodded and sat down. Gwen passed her a plate heaped with turkey and potatoes. Nikki distractedly molded the mashed potatoes into abstract shapes with her fork, wondering how to tell Gwen about Darius.

"Is something wrong?" asked Gwen.

Nikki opened her mouth, then closed it abruptly. She could feel her ears turning red as everyone stared at her.

"It's Mr. Darius," said Curio, his mouth full of turkey. "He's downstairs, with Rufius the Ruffian."

Gwen stared at him, her face turning as white as the whipped cream she was picking off the blueberry pie. "What do you mean Darius is downstairs?" she finally said. "Why would Rufius bring him here? Is he under guard? In chains?"

Curio shook his head. "Nope, no guards or chains, Miss. He's just sitting next to Rufius drinking ale."

Gwen stared from Curio to Nikki.

Nikki tried to give her a reassuring pat on the arm, but Gwen jerked her arm away, knocking over a gravy boat.

They all sat watching the gravy spread across the white tablecloth and down onto the floor.

The Prince finally broke the silence. "Rufius I'm familiar with, unfortunately, but who is Darius?"

"He's Miss Gwen's sweetheart," said Curio.

Gwen's cheeks turned as pink as her cloak, while Fuzz snorted with laughter.

"Ah," said the Prince, tactfully staring down at his plate.

The rasp of a chair being pushed back suddenly broke the silence. Gwen jumped up and headed for the door. Nikki and Fuzz dashed after her.

Nikki plastered herself across the door before Gwen could open it. "Gwen, you can't go down there. Rufius will have you arrested on sight. Do you want to be sent back to the dungeons of the Southern Castle? Forced to make dangerous concoctions and explosives that Rufius will use against the people of the Realm?"

Gwen didn't answer. She just reached around Nikki, trying to get at the door handle.

"I say, Gwennie," said Bertie strolling over as he dabbed at his mouth with a napkin. "If you're in some kind of trouble with that nasty little Rufius fellow then I think your friends are right. You should stay here. The Prince and I will go down and talk to this Darius person. We'll have the matter straightened out in a jiffy."

Gwen didn't respond, but she backed away from the door.

"Is it safe for you to be seen in public?" Nikki asked the Prince of Physics. "The last time we saw you your estate in Kingston was surrounded by the Knights of the Iron Fist."

The Prince waved away her worried look. "Of course," he said. "I'm not in hiding. Quite the contrary. Since I arrived here in Cogent Town yesterday I've been deliberately riding my horse up and down the streets, trying to be seen by as many people as possible. I'm trying to show the people of the Realm that Rufius doesn't control everyone and everything. At least not yet."

"But what about Kingston?" asked Nikki. "Aren't you afraid the knights will take over the city while you're away?"

"No," said the Prince. "The Knights of the Iron Fist aren't driven by politics, or even by power. They fight for whoever pays them, and it seems that Rufius has been neglecting his bribes to them ever since he arrived here in Cogent Town. Communications between Kingston and Cogent Town are a bit slow, but the last I heard the knights have left Kingston and have retreated to a camp somewhere along the south coast. It seems that without an ongoing source of bribes they revert back to their natural state of drunken laziness. Now, Bertie and I will go down and have a little chat with Rufius and Darius to see what's going on. I don't think Rufius will try anything against the King's nephew in such a public place. The rest of you stay here."

The Prince opened the door and Bertie dutifully followed him out of the room, though he looked a bit nervous.

As soon as the door closed Fuzz darted to a corner of the room and pulled out a pocketknife. He knelt on the floor and pushed the knife blade under one of the floorboards. "Blast," he said. "Someone's varnished the floor since the last time I was here. The board's stuck."

Nikki grabbed a butter knife from the table and knelt down by Fuzz. After sawing through the varnish they managed to pry the board loose.

Fuzz set the board to one side, revealing a small round hole two inches wide. "Drilled this myself ten years ago. The King asked me and Athena to keep an eye on a band of thieves which used to meet in this tavern." He put his eye to the hole. "Gives you a good view of the main room. I can see Rufius. Ech, he's drinking glowworm. Vile stuff. I tried it once, and once was enough. Gave me nightmares for a week." He sighed and sat up. "The view is good, but the sound is not. You can only hear through this hole when the tavern is mostly empty. There's just too many people down there today."

"Hang on," said Nikki. She looked around the room. She needed something stiff but flexible, like a piece of cardboard. She walked over to an ugly picture of a buck-toothed little boy hanging on the wall. "This might work," she said, taking the picture down and pulling the canvas away from the frame. She rolled the canvas into a cone shape and put the wide end of the cone over the hole in the floor. Then she put the narrow end into her ear. "Yep," she said. "It's a bit jumbled up with other voices, but if you listen carefully you can just make out Rufius talking. Good thing this hole is right over his table."

"Let me listen," said Fuzz.

Nikki turned the cone over to him and she and Curio sat down at the table while Gwen paced the room.

"So how does that work, Miss?" asked Curio, chewing on a piece of bread while he watched Fuzz. "Don't seem like it would make much difference having that painting in his ear. Mr. Fuzz's ear ain't any closer to Rufius than it was before."

"A cone shape helps focus sound," said Nikki. "It kind of blocks out background noise. The cone shape gathers up sound waves and funnels them into your ear."

"Waves, Miss?" said Curio. "Like waves on the ocean? Don't see how there can be waves washing around this here tavern. People would get all wet."

"Sound waves are like waves in the air, not water waves," said Nikki. "Sound waves are pressure waves, so they're composed of compressions and rarefactions."

Curio just blinked at her.

"Compressions are when the air gets squeezed together," said Nikki, moving her palms together. "And rarefactions are when the air expands." She pulled her palms apart. "So when this squeezing and expanding happens over and over you get a wave travelling through the air. Then that wave goes into your ear and hits your eardrum. That's how you hear sounds."

Curio set his piece of bread down and stared at her. "We have drums in our ears, Miss?" He poked a finger in his ear. "I don't feel nothing except some waxy gunk." He pulled his finger out and showed it to her. It was not only waxy but black.

Nikki grimaced. "Jeez, Curio. When was the last time you washed your ears?"

"Dunno, Miss," said Curio, examining his finger. "None of me gets washed very often."

"Well, if we get safely to the Prince's house you're going to have a bath," said Nikki. "With soap."

Curio shrugged. "If you say so, Miss. Personally, I don't mind a bit of dirt. Kind of used to it, I guess." He looked up from his finger. Fuzz was walking toward them.

"Well, I heard a fair amount of the conversation," he said, sitting down at the table. There was an angry scowl on his face as he motioned Gwen over.

Gwen sat, staring intently at Fuzz.

"The Prince and Rufius did most of the talking," said Fuzz. "A lot of veiled threats were thrown back and forth, but nobody declared outright war. The men around Rufius were fingering their knives and glaring at the Prince, but they were watching for a sign from Rufius and he didn't give it. That doesn't surprise me. The Prince and Rufius have gotten themselves into a standoff. They each have almost equal power in the Realm now. The King, Bertie, and the nobles have whatever power is left. If we're ever going to get rid of Rufius we have to somehow convince the King, Bertie, and the nobility to join with the Prince of Physics. And now is the time to do it. Rufius has made a major mistake in not continuing his bribes to the Knights of the Iron Fist. I think he's gotten cocky. He thinks the people of the Realm are more afraid of him than they actually are. Most of the people in the outlying villages don't even know who he is. They'll continue to follow the King, just out of habit."

He paused and looked over at Gwen with a half angry, half pained expression.

"What?" asked Gwen tensely.

"The face off between the Prince and Rufius was no surprise," said Fuzz. "But what Darius said was." Fuzz's mouth twisted like he'd swallowed something sour. "Darius has joined Rufius because Rufius has promised to push all imps out of the Realm."

Curio gasped. "You mean Mr. Darius is a Remover?"
Fuzz nodded.

"What's a Remover?" asked Nikki. "You don't mean that he wants all imps killed, do you?" she asked, looking sick. "I don't see how that can be. He helped rescue Athena's Aunt Gertie and the other imps from the Southern Castle. And he helped when Rufius and the Knights of the Iron Fist invaded ImpHaven."

"Removers don't want the imps killed," said Fuzz. "They just want them removed from the Realm. Removers are obsessed with everyone in the Realm being the same. To their minds the imps don't fit in, even though we've been here for centuries."

"Well that's almost as bad," said Nikki, still shocked. "I mean, of course that's not as bad as killing, but still. It's very nasty and I just can't believe that Darius would think like that. Maybe he's acting. You know, pretending to be one these Removers to fool Rufius. So he can get close to Rufius and learn his plans."

Gwen slowly shook her head. "No," she said, her face gray. "No, he's not pretending. He said something to me, back in ImpHaven. We were taking a walk in the garden of Athena's mother's house. At the time I was confused by what he meant, but now I understand." She looked down at her hands. "He said that once the land was cleared the Realm would be a better place to live. I thought he was talking about farmland being cleared, which was odd as he's not a farmer."

"Yeah, Removers talk like that," said Fuzz. "Clearing the land, making everything pure. And it's not just the imps they want gone. They aren't too keen on people from the Southern Isles either. I hope your friend Kira is being careful or she might find herself sent back to her home island. There are a lot of Removers here in Cogent Town. They like to stay close to the castle, to be near the seat of power." Fuzz sighed. "Well, let's not get ahead of ourselves. Right now we need to focus on getting safely to the Prince's house here in town. His carriage is probably our best bet. It's parked out back, in the alley behind the tavern." He cut himself a slice of ham and stared thoughtfully down at the table while he ate.

Gwen started pacing the room again. Curio dished himself up a huge piece of blueberry pie and soon added blue teeth to his black ears.

Nikki wandered over to the hole in the floor and removed the canvas cone. She knelt down and put her eye to the hole. Rufius and the Prince were still talking. The Prince was standing, arms folded. Rufius lounged in his chair, sipping his glowing green drink. Occasionally he made a remark, but mainly he just sat back and watched, as if the Prince was a court jester sent to amuse him. Nikki's gaze wandered to the other men sitting at the table. She didn't recognize any of them. None were knights, or at least they weren't in armor. They all had a shifty, shabby look to them, as if they belonged to a gang of pickpockets. She twisted her neck to get a look at the people standing near the table. "Oh no!" she whispered.

"What is it?" demanded Fuzz, running up to her.

"Lurker," said Nikki, pointing at the hole with a shaking hand.

"Let me see," said Fuzz, kneeling down next to her.

"Is it the same one what followed us out of Border Town, Miss?" asked Curio. "I thought we left him far behind cause of our Kite Cart."

"Yes, it's the same one," said Nikki. "He's got that red scar across his face. He chased us through Linnea's village, and he was watching us when we were in Gwen's backyard in Deceptionville. When Gwen set off that explosion to demonstrate her gunpowder. I'm sure he's the one that told Rufius about the gunpowder."

"It's not gunpowder," Gwen said quietly. "My intent is to see if it can be useful in mining, or possibly in tunnel-making."

"Ssshh!" hissed Fuzz, his ear to the hole. "Rufius is saying something I can't quite catch. Something about a dam. It sounds important." He listened for a few minutes, but finally sat up, shaking his head. "Can't hear anymore. There's a big crowd of drinkers at the next table playing dice and yelling loud enough to rattle the windows."

Nikki knelt down and looked through the hole again. Rufius and the Prince were still talking. Bertie was trying to talk to Darius, but Darius just folded his arms and ignored him. Nikki twisted her neck again, scanning the room. "Oh no!" she gasped, sitting up.

"What?" said Fuzz.

"The Lurker's not there anymore," said Nikki.

Fuzz immediately ran to the door. He carefully opened it a crack and peered out. "No one there," he said, quietly closing it again. "It's possible the Lurker's left the tavern, but it's never a good idea to assume that a Lurker has lost your trail. I'd bet my last gold coin that he's searching the tavern for anyone who might have come in with the Prince." He grabbed a small rucksack off the table and shooed everyone toward the door. "We need to get out of here now. We can't wait for the Prince and Bertie to come back."

"But how are we going to get out of the tavern without being seen?" asked Nikki. "The stairs lead right into the main room. They're sure to spot us. Especially Gwen. She sticks out a mile, even without that pink cloak."

"We're not going down the stairs," said Fuzz, motioning to Gwen to hand over her cloak.

Gwen gave it to him and he ran to a window and dropped the cloak into the street.

"Everybody out," said Fuzz as he opened the door.

They filed quietly out and waited in the hallway as Fuzz held up a finger. He tiptoed to the stairs leading down to the second floor and listened intently. "All clear so far," he whispered. "This way." He led them to a broom closet. Its door was ajar and buckets and mops were piled inside. A short length of rope was dangling from the ceiling. "Pull on that rope," Fuzz whispered to Gwen, who was the tallest.

Gwen reached up and yanked on the rope. There was a loud screech as a trapdoor opened above their heads and a rope ladder swung down. Fuzz and Curio scrambled quickly up the ladder. Gwen had a bit more trouble as she kept stepping on her long silk dress. Nikki followed her and tried as best she could to lift the hem of Gwen's dress with one hand while climbing with the other. When they had all reached the top Fuzz pulled the trapdoor up after them. They were in a storage shed. Pots of paint and roofing tar were stacked against the walls. Fuzz opened a door and they all blinked as he led them out into bright sunlight.

"We're on the roof," said Curio. "I can see the castle." He pointed at the marble turrets of Castle Cogent gleaming in the distance. Its purple and gold flags were flapping in the breeze.

"Yes," said Fuzz. "Stay away from the edge. I don't want anyone down in the street spotting your little purple cap. They'll call the Rounders to investigate." He headed to the far side of the roof and carefully poked his head over the side. "The Prince's carriage is parked in the alley right below us."

Nikki joined him and looked over the edge. The carriage filled the alley, with barely a foot of space on either side of it. Two magnificent black horses were harnessed to it. The carriage appeared to be unguarded. No driver or groom was in sight.

Gwen and Curio joined them. "How're we gonna get down there?" asked Curio. "Don't see nothing we can climb down on."

"There should be ropes up here somewhere," said Fuzz. "For the window washers or the men who tar the roof. Or we can use the rope ladder we climbed up, though I don't think that'll be long enough." He and Curio went to search for ropes while Nikki and Gwen stared down at the top of the carriage.

"It's made of leather," said Gwen. "High quality, and quite thick by the look of it."

"Yes," said Nikki. She leaned over farther, eyeing the walls of the tavern. "How high up would you say we are?"

"About thirty feet I'd guess," said Gwen. "Maybe forty."

Nikki nodded. "It's a little higher than I'd like, but I think it will work."

"Yes," said Gwen. "We can lower Fuzz and Curio down so they'll have less distance to fall. You and I can climb over the edge and hang from our fingers before falling."

Curio returned. "No ropes anywhere," he said. "Mr. Fuzz is sawing at that rope ladder with his little pocketknife, but the Lurker'll probably find us before he's done."

"That's okay," said Nikki. "We're going to jump. Go get Fuzz."

"Are you sure this is a good idea?" asked Fuzz as he joined them. "If we're captured by Lurkers I can probably get us out of the castle dungeon with a few well-placed bribes, payed for by

Bertie. But I can't do much if we break out necks."

"We'll be okay," said Nikki in what she hoped was a confident voice. "Leather is strong and it has a lot of give. We'll bounce as if we're on a trampoline."

"A what?" asked Gwen.

"Never mind," said Nikki. "Fuzz, you're the lightest. You should go first."

The look Fuzz gave her was none too happy, but he nodded and eased himself over the edge of the roof. Nikki and Gwen grabbed his wrists and lowered him down as far as they could. Nikki held her breath as they let go.

Fuzz seemed to fall for a long time. When he hit the roof of the carriage he bounced high into the air.

The rebound was much larger than Nikki had anticipated. She winced as Fuzz bounced sideways into the wall of the tavern. He looked a bit shaken when the bouncing finally stopped, but he waved at them and climbed down the back of the carriage.

"Try to bend your knees when you hit," Nikki said to Curio as they dangled him over the edge of the roof. "You won't bounce as high."

"Yes, Miss," said Curio, his voice quavering.

Curio's drop was more successful. He landed on his feet, bent his knees, and looked like a gymnast landing a perfect vault. He quickly scrambled off the carriage roof to join Fuzz in the alley.

"I'm heaviest," said Gwen. "I'll go last. I don't want to risk damaging the roof before your jump."

Nikki gave Gwen a quick hug and inched over the edge. She made the mistake of looking down before jumping. Now that she was dangling by her fingertips the drop seemed a lot farther. Just as she let go she heard a crashing sound up on the roof. She hit the top of the carriage on her back and bounced like she was on a springy mattress. She could see Gwen's head poking over the edge of the roof, and to her horror she also saw the black-hooded shape of a Lurker suddenly loom up behind Gwen. Gwen disappeared from sight and the sounds of a scuffle came from the rooftop.

Fuzz's head appeared over the edge of the carriage roof. "Get down quick!" he hissed. "Into the carriage!"

Nikki scrambled off the leather roof and followed Curio inside while Fuzz climbed up onto the coachman's seat. Fuzz flicked the reins and the carriage jolted forward, its heavy wooden wheels scrapping the tavern wall as it careened around a corner and out of the alley.

Nikki leaned out the carriage window to see what had become of Gwen, but the tavern was already out of sight. "We have to go back!" she yelled at Fuzz. "Gwen's still on the roof and I saw a Lurker up there!"

"I know," yelled Fuzz, steering around a cart full of bright orange pumpkins. "I saw him too. But there's nothing we can do to help Gwen right now. Once we're safe inside the Prince's house we'll try to come up with a rescue plan."

Nikki contemplated jumping out of the carriage and running back to help Gwen, but they were on a main road now and Fuzz had the horses dashing along at a gallop. Throwing herself out onto the cobblestones at this pace would definitely mean broken bones. Nikki sat back on the seat and hung on as the carriage bounced and creaked as if it was going to break apart.

"There's horses following us, Miss," said Curio. He was kneeling on the seat and peering out a small back window.

Nikki twisted around and looked out. Four horses were galloping along the road behind them, their riders whipping them to faster and faster speeds. "Fuzz, we're being followed," she yelled. "They're gaining on us."

"I can hear them," yelled Fuzz. "Just sit tight. The Prince's mansion isn't far. It's on the edge of town, at the end of this road. He always has armed guards stationed in his grounds. The guards will be able to hold off whoever's following us."

Nikki watched anxiously as the four horses came closer and closer. She didn't recognize any of the riders. The Lurker wasn't among them. He was probably dragging Gwen off to the dungeons of Castle Cogent. At least it was unlikely that Gwen would be hurt. Rufius would want her alive to create gunpowder and other weapons. Nikki tried not to think about what might happen if Gwen refused.

"We're here!" Fuzz suddenly shouted. The carriage jerked to an abrupt halt, throwing Nikki and Curio to the floor. They scrambled out as Fuzz jumped down from the coachman's seat.

"Open up!" Fuzz yelled, banging with his fists on a massive iron gate set into a high stone wall.

The gate creaked slowly open just as their four followers charged up and dismounted from their horses.

"I'm Fuzz, the King's emissary," Fuzz yelled at the spear-carrying guards who had opened the gate. "I'm a friend of the Prince and seek sanctuary in his house."

The guards looked uncertainly from Fuzz to the four riders standing menacingly behind him.

"Well, don't just stand there gawking. Let them in," said a voice from inside the grounds.

Nikki recognized the pompous voice at once. It was Morton, the Prince's Head Butler. As he stepped forward she could see he was wearing the same green satin tailcoat that he'd been wearing in Kingston, when she'd arrived with Griff's crew at the Prince's estate.

"Morton, you old rascal," said Fuzz, shoving Nikki and Curio through the gate. "Good to see you!"

"Master Fuzz," said Morton, inclining his head slightly. "Up to your old tricks again I see." He waved imperiously at the guards. "Shut the gate."

The four riders darted forward, but beat a hasty retreat when the guards lowered their spears and looked ready to charge.

The gate clanged shut and the sound of horses galloping away echoed along the street.

Nikki looked around her. The grounds of the Prince's Cogent Town mansion were much smaller than his estate in Kingston. There were no apple orchards or vegetable gardens. The house was smaller too. It was a two-story white marble mansion set in a rose garden over-shadowed by tall fir and hemlock trees. The house was similar in design to the mansion of the Duchess of Falsa, with carved marble balconies overlooking the street from the second floor. But the Prince's house had no lilac bushes, footmen, or violin music wafting from the windows. The tall fir trees gave the whole place a shadowy and gloomy feeling. An alabaster fountain in the shape of a graceful nymph splashed in the shadows and blue hyacinths glowed in the half-light like flowery candles.

Morton led them up the front stairs and into a mirrored foyer. "Excuse me while I see to it that your rooms are prepared," he said. "A friend of yours is in the back parlor. Please join her there and I'll have the cook send in afternoon tea."

Chapter Three

✦

A Strange Alliance

WHEN THEY ENTERED the parlor a small figure rose from an armchair in front of a roaring fire.

"Athena!" gasped Nikki, running forward and enveloping the imp in a joyous hug.

"Yes, Miss, it is me," said Athena, giving Nikki a reassuring pat on the back. She swayed a little and Nikki quickly helped her back into the armchair.

"How's your leg?" asked Nikki.

"It is better, Miss," said Athena, primly arranging the long skirt of her gray woolen dress. "The Prince had his own healer attend to it. The redness and swelling have gone down, and I shall soon be able to walk again. He applied poultices of honey and oregano oil to the wound and they have helped a great deal, though I admit I am not fond of smelling like a tossed salad. The healer also had me eat a piece of very moldy bread, which I must say I was very reluctant to do. I wish Miss Linnea had been here to advise me. She is such an expert healer and would have known whether eating mold was a good treatment or not."

"Oh my gosh!" said Nikki. "Penicillin!"

"I beg your pardon, Miss?" said Athena.

"It's not important," said Nikki. "It's just that we have a

treatment that uses mold, back where I come from. It can cure certain types of infection caused by bacteria. Though I think the mold has to be processed and purified in some way. I don't think just eating moldy bread will help much. I'm guessing that it was the honey that helped with your infection. There's pretty good evidence that honey can kill bacteria."

"What's bacteria, Miss?" asked Curio, plopping down on the rug in front of the fire.

"They're like tiny little animals that are too small to see. They can cause wounds to become infected."

Curio's mouth dropped open and his eyes became as wide as saucers. He peered intently at a small scratch on his arm. "Do they have nasty claws that dig into you?" he asked, poking a dirty fingernail into the scratch.

"No, no. Don't worry about that scratch. It's too small to become infected. Anyway, never mind about the bacteria," said Nikki. "They're too hard to explain and I'd need a microscope to show them to you. The Prince might have one here in the house, but we have more important things to discuss. Like how to rescue Gwen."

"Why? What has happened to Miss Gwendolyn?" asked Athena.

"Lurker," said Fuzz, sitting down in the armchair facing her. "He snatched her at the Fox and Fig. We were meeting with Bertie and the Prince in one of the tavern's upper rooms when Rufius showed up downstairs with a bunch of his followers. There was a Lurker among them. The same one who's been following us all over the Realm. Looks like he's Rufius's pet. The three of us got away in the Prince's carriage, but Gwen wasn't so lucky. He took quite a risk, grabbing a Duchess's daughter. The nobility will be up in arms about it when the news gets around. I'm sure the Lurker was acting on Rufius's orders, but I'm not sure what

Rufius wants her for. Maybe as a hostage."

"*I* know why Rufius wants the young lady," said a voice by the parlor door.

They all turned.

Nikki, Fuzz, and Curio gasped in astonishment at the sight of the woman who approached them, but Athena appeared unsurprised and only grimaced as if she'd eaten something sour.

Fortuna the Fortunate, her long, grayish-black hair tangling in her many amber necklaces and multi-colored scarves, sat down heavily on a padded footstool next to Athena's chair.

Athena gritted her teeth and inched away from her.

"What on earth?" Fuzz finally gasped, looking at Athena.

"Fortuna has some information which may be of help to us," Athena said through clenched teeth. "The Prince is letting her stay in his house as long as her behavior is civil."

Fortuna cackled through her crooked teeth. "Better be nice to me, Miss Prissy. Rufius has big plans, plans which I know all about. Plans which I'll only reveal after I've been showered in gold coins."

"The Prince has already informed you that he will pay you well, if your information is useful," said Athena.

Fortuna snorted. "Paying me well won't do, dearie. Paying me lots and lots and lots is what I require."

"I thought you already had piles of gold coins," said Nikki. "From your sales of Lily of the Night and Panther's Pride, back in Deceptionville. Or didn't Panther's Pride cure baldness quite as well as you said it would?"

Fortuna's black eyes flashed with anger. "You'd do well to hold your tongue, young lady. Yes, I recognize you despite that ridiculous page's outfit. I'll never forgive you for ruining my Fish Fortunes. They were bringing in a healthy amount of coin until you showed up on the Isle of Ignorance and practically forced me to do that ridiculous weather prediction. The local idiots stopped paying for my Fish Fortunes the very next day. But I'll have you know that Panther's Pride is still selling quite well. The world will never run out of men who are losing their hair. The trick is to make sure you get their coin before they realize how long the potion may take to work."

"What about Lily of the Night?" asked Nikki. "Did it make all the old ladies in Deceptionville look twenty again?"

Fortuna airily waved away the question. "There was a slight problem with that potion. Apparently it can cause mild burns on the face. The pursuit of beauty can be painful at times. One would have thought that burns on the face would be a small price to pay for looking like a young girl again, but apparently the women of D-ville are unable to bear even the smallest discomfort."

Athena, glaring at Fortuna, was about to speak when the sound of heavy footsteps came from the open parlor door.

Bertie and the Prince of Physics strode into the room.

"Bertie!" Athena gasped. "Oh my goodness! It has been such a long time since I last saw you. You were such a small little boy. But look at you now. So tall and handsome."

Bertie laughed and bent down to plant a kiss on Athena's cheek. "It's lovely to see you again, dearest Athena. It must be ten years or more since we last met. But I gather that you and Fuzz are still up to your old intrigues."

"I am the King's emissary," said Athena with a touch of her old haughtiness. "I do not engage in intrigues. We are doing important work. We are striving to save the Realm from an evil man who is trying to take over your uncle's throne."

"Yes," said Bertie, gloom coming over his usually cheerful face. "I've met the evil man you're referring to. More of a boy, really. Barely past school age. It's hard to believe that such a youngster can be a threat to the Realm."

"Don't be fooled by his youth," said the Prince, standing next to Fuzz's chair with his arms folded across his black velvet tunic. "He has a loathsome type of cunning and a talent with bribes that have attracted many followers."

"That's where you come in Bertie," said Fuzz. "We need some followers of our own and you're going to get them for us."

"Me?" said Bertie, looking alarmed. "Of course, I'm always happy to help out old friends. You and Athena can ask me anything. But you know I'm not one for palace intrigues. I've always kept well away from such things. And besides, I've been away from the Realm for years. People have probably forgotten all about me."

"No they haven't," said Fuzz. "Most of the courtiers up at the castle and the majority of the nobility here in Cogent Town will welcome you back with open arms. You're the successor to the throne. Keeping the throne in the royal family is very important to the nobles. Since most of them are distantly related to the royal family it gives them access to power so long as either your uncle or you are King. It's true that some of the courtiers are in Rufius's pocket. He's been handing out bribes right and left up at the castle. But he's counting on their greed while forgetting about their snobbery. They'll take his money, but they can't stand that he's only the son of a cheese monger. He's got zero noble blood and we can use that to our advantage."

"So what is your plan, exactly?" asked Bertie. "You want me to talk to the nobles? Declare my intention of accepting the throne if my uncle dies? Hand out bribes of my own?"

"All of the above," said Fuzz.

"Dear me," said Bertie, turning pale and tugging at the tight collar of his silk tunic. "All of this sounds like a rather dangerous enterprise. This chap Rufius may not be much a threat on his own, but he has quite the retinue around him. There was an actual Lurker among his cronies at the Fox and Fig. He stared at me the whole time the Prince and I were conversing with Rufius. It made me quite nervous. I never could stand those Lurker chaps. Don't know why my uncle employs them."

"His Highness does *not* employ the Lurkers," Athena said sternly. "They were hired and trained by Maleficious as spies and assassins. Rufius, who has taken on Maleficious's role as advisor to the King, now commands the Lurkers."

"Ah," said Bertie, still pale and sweaty. "Well, that is definitely not encouraging. What about the Rounders? They're quite a large group of men and well-armed. It's all very well to try to get a few nobles to join us, but if the Rounders are against us we don't stand a chance. They'll just arrest us all and throw us in the deepest part of the castle dungeons."

"The Rounders are loyal to the King," said Fuzz. "There may be a few here and there who've taken Rufius's bribes, but most are quite loyal to the throne. No, we don't need to worry about the Rounders. If worst comes to worst and armed conflict breaks out the Rounders will rally to the King. The armed group we *do* need to worry about is the Knights of the Iron Fist. They're very much under Rufius's control, as long as he keeps bribing them with lots of gold. Right now my informants tell me they're hanging out in one of their camps on the southern coast, near Kingston. They're currently in an undisciplined mood, drinking ale all night and sleeping all day. They've pulled most of their knights out of Kingston except for a small group still watching the Prince's estate."

"Yes," said the Prince. "Their forces in Kingston and in the Southern Castle are greatly reduced. I had no trouble traveling here to Cogent Town. The knights watching my estate let me and my retinue leave without attempting to stop us. And we met none of them on the road as we traveled here. My guess is that they've gotten bored. They've lost interest in bullying the townsfolk in Kingston and the farmers in the countryside. They've never been a very disciplined force. They're more bandits than knights. Which is actually a good thing for our side. If we can pay them more than Rufius does then they won't be a threat anymore. We'll be able to convince them to sit on the sidelines and not fight if Rufius makes a move to take over the King's throne."

A sudden loud cackle from Fortuna made everyone jump.

"Lurkers! Rounders! Armed knights!" she said, slapping her knee and laughing hysterically. "None of these nincompoops matter even the tiniest bit. None of them are part of Rufius's plan to take over the Realm. Nope, not part of his glorious plan. His wonderful, foolproof plan. His very well plotted and detailed plan. And who knows these details? I'll give you two guesses." She playfully swung one of her amber necklaces around her fingers.

"Madame, if you have knowledge about Rufius's plans I insist that you share it at once," said the Prince.

Fortuna just smirked at him.

"You said you know why Rufius wants Gwen," said Nikki. "You could at least tell us that."

Fortuna shook her head, sending her beaded necklaces clacking against each other. "Nope. Not until I get my gold. Lots and lots of lovely gold."

"So Gwen is part of this big plan of Rufius's that you're talking about?" asked Nikki.

Fortuna rubbed her thumb and index finger together in the universal sign for money.

The Prince of Physics sighed and abruptly strode out of the room. He returned a few minutes later carrying a jingling canvas bag which he dropped in Fortuna's lap.

Fortuna opened the bag and thrust her hand inside. She pulled out a fistful of shiny gold coins, glinting in the firelight. "This'll do for a start, dearies," she said, dropping the coins back into the bag. "Rufius wants Lady Ursula's daughter, the tall blond one, because she knows how to make black powder. The same black powder that blew such a huge hole in the wall of the Southern Castle."

"What is Rufius going to use this black powder for?" asked the Prince of Physics.

Fortuna chortled. "Well, that's the crux of the matter, isn't it my dear? The details of that will cost you more than this one puny little bag of coins." She lifted the bag up as if weighing it. "I'd say ten more of these bags should extract the full tale from me."

Bertie gasped. "I say, that's asking for quite a lot madam. I'll wager there isn't that much gold in all of Cogent Town."

"Oh, but there is dearie," said Fortuna. "The castle treasury holds enough gold to satisfy even little me."

"But, we can't just waltz up to the castle and ask my uncle to open the treasury," said Bertie. "He won't do it. Not even for me. Do *you* have that much money?" he asked the Prince.

The Prince shook his head. "No. Not here in this house. I could possibly raise it by selling one of my properties. I own several farms near Cogent Town. But that would take time."

"I don't think we *have* time," said Fuzz. "From the rumors I've been hearing around town Rufius is moving quickly. He's going to try to seize power very soon."

Everyone was quiet. Athena closed her eyes, Fuzz stared into the fire, and Nikki stared down at the carpet, trying to think of something that would help.

"Well," said Fortuna, breaking the silence. "If you're all going to just sit here like useless lumps then I'm going up to my room.

Send one of the maids up with a nice afternoon tea. I want scones with butter and a pile of fat cream-cakes." She heaved herself off the padded footstool and flounced from the room.

Chapter Four

A Bit of Burglary

"A RE YOU SURE this is going to work, Miss?" whispered Curio, sitting with his knees pulled up to his chin.

"It'll work," whispered Nikki with more confidence than she felt. She peered through a slit in the tablecloth, watching Geber's sandals and the bottom of his cane slowly pass in front of the table they were hiding under. It had been surprisingly easy to slip into Geber's workroom in Castle Cogent without being seen. Their page uniforms still rendered them practically invisible, and Sandor, Geber's assistant, was nowhere in sight. The old alchemist himself was so deaf and nearsighted that he hadn't even noticed them slink into the room and dart under the table.

Nikki and Curio had been the obvious candidates for this mission to the castle. Gwen was still missing, Athena's leg was still too painful for her to walk, Bertie and the Prince would have attracted too much attention, and as an imp Fuzz was finding it harder and harder to move easily around Cogent Town. Gangs of Removers were now openly harassing imps on the streets.

Nikki listened closely, trying to figure out what Geber was doing. She could hear him muttering to himself but couldn't make out the words. She had just resigned herself to a long wait when she suddenly heard Geber shuffle across the workroom's creaky wooden floor. The door slammed shut and a key turned in the lock. She cautiously poked her head out from under the tablecloth. The door of the workroom was shut and Geber was gone. She crawled out from under the table and brushed the dust off her page uniform. The fact that Geber had locked the door from the outside was possibly a hitch in their plan, but she'd worry about that later. One problem at a time.

Curio crawled out and glanced at all the shelves lining the walls. "Gosh, there's lots of bottles and potions here, Miss. Do you know which ones we need?"

"Kind of," said Nikki. The goal of their mission was to steal enough gold from the castle treasury to satisfy Fortuna. Fuzz had told them that the castle treasury wasn't usually guarded. Instead it had many, many thick iron bars and massive iron locks on its gates. It had never been broken into. Not in all the centuries since Castle Cogent had been built.

Nikki went over to a shelf nailed to the back wall between the room's arched windows. The shelf held twenty or so glass bottles with cork stoppers, all carefully labelled. The problem was that the Realm didn't use the same names for things that her modern world back home did. She was looking for acids which would burn through the iron bars and locks of the treasury. Hydrochloric acid would be the best choice, but none of the glass bottles were conveniently labelled 'hydrochloric acid'. Instead they were labelled things like 'Silver Serpent Venom' and 'Blood of Bat Tongue'. Geber seemed to have a fondness for colorful and unhelpful names.

She pulled the bottle of Blood of Bat Tongue off the shelf and removed its stopper. The bottle held a clear liquid which didn't look anything like blood. She gave it a cautious sniff. It didn't smell like blood either. More like rubbing alcohol. She sighed. Finding the right bottle wasn't going to be easy. She supposed they could try making their own hydrochloric acid. In her chemistry class back home in Wisconsin they'd made hydrochloric acid by mixing vinegar and salt in a beaker. The acetic acid and water in the vinegar mixed with the chloride in the salt to produce hydrochloric acid. But that method only produced a very weak acid. Much too weak to dissolve iron bars. They didn't have time to make large quantities and then distill it down to a concentrated solution. No, they were going to have to make do with what Geber had already created.

"See if you can find a stone bowl," she said to Curio. "I'll look for something made of iron."

After short search Curio found a stone mortar and pestle and Nikki dug up a rusty iron stirrup from the bottom of an old wooden trunk full of clothes. Nikki cleared a space on one of Geber's workbenches and set the stone mortar down. She put the iron stirrup inside it and set the most likely bottles in a row on the workbench.

The liquid from the first bottle she tried did nothing at all to the iron. The second one bubbled a bit but did no damage. There were no promising reactions until the tenth bottle. That liquid created a small hole in the stirrup.

"Sulfuric acid," said Nikki, sniffing carefully. "But it's too diluted to be useful. It would take days to melt through a big iron bar with this. And we don't have time to distill it to a stronger solution." She put the stopper back in the bottle. "Put these back and get some more bottles."

They went through a whole wall of shelves before they finally found it. One tiny drop of 'Devil's Fire' melted through the iron stirrup as if it was a stick of butter. Nikki re-stoppered it, being careful not to get any of the liquid on her hands. The faint vinegary odor of hydrochloric acid wafted in the air. She set the bottle down and went over to the old wooden chest where she'd found the stirrup. After a bit of digging she unearthed a leather saddlebag and a linen shirt. She wrapped the bottle in the linen and carefully tucked it into the bag.

"There," she said. "That should keep it from breaking. Come on. Let's get out of here." She took a last look around to make sure everything was back where they'd found it. A piece of fabric was sticking out from the lid of the wooden trunk. She tucked it back inside. "Okay. I think we're ready to tackle the next problem."

"What's that, Miss?" asked Curio.

"The door's locked," said Nikki.

Curio darted forward and tried the door. After leaning back and pulling on it with both hands had no effect he bent and looked through the keyhole. "Mr. Geber's taken the key with him, Miss. I was hoping maybe it was still in the lock. We might've been able to push it out of the keyhole. I did that once when me master locked me in his cellar. It popped right out and clattered on the floor. Master heard the noise, but I dodged him and climbed out the kitchen window. Had a nice roam around D-ville for a couple of days. Three days of doing no work was very nice, but when you don't work you don't eat so I had to go back to him."

As usual Nikki had no adequate response to the awful tales of Curio's childhood, so she just patted him on the shoulder and bent to take a look at the keyhole. She could see all the way through to the hallway outside Geber's workroom. It was very frustrating to see freedom without being able to reach it. She pulled on the door but had no more success than Curio had.

"We could melt the lock, Miss," said Curio. "Now that we've got that there Devil's Fire stuff."

"Yeah," said Nikki, "but that would announce that someone's been in here. Geber or Sandor might be back any minute.

They'd see the melted lock and call the castle guards. And we don't know how long it'll take us to get into the treasury. It'd be better not to leave any trace. That'll give us more time to get the gold and escape from the castle."

"Well, that just leaves the windows, Miss," said Curio.

They went over to the two arched windows and peered out. The workroom was at the top level of Castle Cogent, hundreds of feet up from the rocky crag the castle sat on. The smooth white marble walls of the castle dropped below them without so much as a single foothold.

Curio opened the latch of one window and pushed it open. He leaned out and looked up. "You might not like this idea, Miss. Don't know how you feel about heights. But look." He pointed upward.

Nikki joined him and looked where he was pointing. "Oh," she said, feeling her legs already beginning to tremble. She wasn't really very afraid of heights. Normally they didn't bother her much. But they were very high up. One slip and there was no way they'd survive such a fall.

"Do you think it will hold, Miss?" asked Curio. "It looks pretty sturdy."

"Yes, I think it will hold," said Nikki, her shoulders sagging. "Well, if we're going to do it we'd better do it right now, before we have time to think about it. I saw a coil of rope at the bottom of that old wooden chest." She handed Curio the leather saddlebag containing the bottle of hydrochloric acid and retrieved the rope from the chest. She tied a large loop in one end of the rope and took a few practice swings with it. Her mother had once taken her to a rodeo in the small town of Manawa, Wisconsin. The cowboys in the calf-roping event had caught steers by throwing a loop of rope over their horns. This was kind of similar except she'd have to throw the rope up instead of forward.

She leaned out of the window again and looked up. Her target was a thick iron bracket holding an unlit lantern. Geber's workroom was a long way up from the ground, but it was very close to the top of the castle. A walkway ran along the top of the castle and every ten feet there was an iron bracket and lantern bolted to the marble wall. If they could climb up to the lantern they could easily scramble onto the walkway. The trick of course was not to fall hundreds of feet to the rocky crag below.

"Okay," said Nikki. "Let's do this before I lose my nerve. You'll go first. We can't climb with the bottle of acid. If it slams against the wall while we're climbing it could break and the acid will burn right through us. Once you're safely up on the walkway I'll tie the saddlebag to the rope and you can pull it up."

Curio nodded, a bead of sweat running down his forehead and dropping off his nose.

Nikki leaned out of the window again, took a quick look up and down to make sure no one was watching, then swung the rope a few times to give it some momentum. She let go on the fourth swing. It missed the lantern by a foot. She tried again. And again. On the sixth try the loop finally went over the lantern. Nikki pulled down hard on the rope, hanging all her weight on it. The iron bracket holding the lantern didn't even creak.

"It'll definitely hold our weight," she said. "Just take your time and don't look down. It's not a long climb up. Maybe twenty feet."

Curio took a deep breath and wiped his hands on his velvet page's jacket.

"Wait," said Nikki. She went over to a shelf which held rows of little clay pots. It didn't take long to find what she wanted. "Hold out your hands," she said, scooping a bit of white powder from one of the pots. "Talcum powder. It'll keep your hands from slipping."

Nikki rubbed some of the powder into her own palms and put the pot back on the shelf.

"Here I go, Miss," said Curio in a voice which only shook a little bit. He grabbed the rope with both hands and climbed over the windowsill.

Nikki was startled to see that he had his eyes tightly closed as he pushed away from the window, but it didn't seem to impede his climbing ability. He wrapped both legs around the rope and slowly inched upward. When he reached the lantern he banged his head against it, but by pulling on the iron bracket with one hand and stretching one leg he managed to clamber awkwardly over the low parapet and onto the walkway on top of the castle wall.

Nikki breathed a sigh of relief and quickly tied the saddlebag to the end of the rope. She waved to Curio, who was peering over the parapet. He slowly pulled up the saddlebag and then let down the rope.

Voices from outside in the hallway caused Nikki to freeze, her heart banging in her chest, but the voices passed by without stopping. Nikki quickly grabbed the dangling rope and carefully eased herself off the windowsill. A small creak sounded from the bracket above her head but she determinedly ignored it. Before starting her climb she carefully eased the window shut with her foot until she felt it latch. A sudden impulse to look down gripped her but she gritted her teeth and stared fixedly at the white marble wall inches from her nose. She copied Curio's climbing style, wrapping both legs around the rope and inching upward very slowly.

"Watch your head, Miss," Curio whispered from above.

Nikki glanced up. She had reached the iron bracket. She felt a moment of panic when she realized she'd have to let go of the rope. She hung there, the rope swinging slightly.

"It's not that bad, Miss," whispered Curio. "It's just yer mind playing tricks. Keep one hand on the rope and get a good grip on the lantern with the other. Kinda wrap your whole arm around it. Then just swing your leg up."

The next thing Nikki knew she was kneeling on the walkway, breathing hard. She'd taken a page out of Curio's book and closed her eyes tightly for the scramble over the parapet. She felt Curio pat her on the shoulder.

"All clear, Miss. No guards on this part of the walkway. I'll just pull the rope up."

Nikki got shakily to her feet and looked around. The wide marble walkway on top of the wall was empty except for a few pigeons cooing softly. Castle Cogent was by far the tallest building in Cogent Town and it was also perched high up on it rocky crag. So there was no worry about anyone spotting them from above. It was just guard patrols they had to worry about. Their page uniforms wouldn't save them up here. She very much doubted that pages were allowed up on the walkway. She took the rope that Curio had un-looped from the lantern. "We'll take this," she said, winding it into a coil. "It might come in handy."

Curio nodded and picked up the saddlebag. "I think we should go that way, Miss," he said, pointing at a turret jutting out from one corner of the castle. "I've never been up here, but I think the treasury is in that direction."

As they hurried toward the turret Nikki glanced over the other side of the parapet. She could see a tiny piece of the castle's inner courtyard, many stories down. The green lawn and the rose garden where they'd watched Geber give his crossbow demonstration glowed in the morning sun.

"Get down, Miss!" Curio suddenly whispered, pulling on her arm.

Nikki crouched down beside him. A faint clank of armor

echoed along the walkway. She cautiously peered over the parapet. A guard was patrolling the top of the castle. He was on the other side of the courtyard, but headed their way.

Curio quickly crawled toward the turret, the saddlebag looped over his shoulder. Nikki followed. On their hands and knees they were below the height of the low parapet wall and hidden from sight. They reached the turret without hearing any shouts from the guard. Crawling inside they found an empty round space with arrow holes for the guards to shoot out of. Someone had left a pile of chicken bones and a moldy loaf of bread on the floor. Probably the remains of a guard's lunch. Next to the chicken bones a stone staircase spiraled down into darkness.

Curio started down the staircase but slipped on the top step and would have fallen if Nikki hadn't grabbed him by the collar of his jacket.

"Thank you, Miss," Curio whispered in a shaking voice. "Nearly went head-over-heels. These here marble steps are very slippy."

"Give me the saddlebag," Nikki whispered. "I don't want you burned with acid if you fall."

"I don't think so, Miss," Curio whispered, a hint of stubbornness in his voice. "You're more important to this here mission. Me, I'm just along as a helper." He started down the staircase again.

Nikki swore under her breath. She'd never forgive herself if something happened to Curio, but she couldn't very well pull the saddlebag off of him. She might break the bottle of acid by accident. She could hear the clanking of the guard's armor getting louder. Taking a deep breath to calm her nerves she followed Curio down into the darkness.

The stairs wound down and down without a single torch or

window to light the way. There was no bannister to hang onto and every few minutes one of them would gasp as they slipped and caught themselves just in time. The guards must have another way to reach the walkway on top of the castle walls, Nikki thought. No one would go up or down these stairs each day. They'd have a broken neck in a week. By the time she glimpsed a small ray of torchlight down below Nikki felt like they'd been on the stairs for hours.

"Oh my gosh, Miss," gasped Curio as they finally reached the bottom step of the spiral staircase. "That was an unpleasant time of it and no mistake. Those stairs seemed to go on forever. And each step as slippy as a greased eel."

"Yes," said Nikki, sitting down next to him on the bottom step to catch her breath. The stairs had come out in an underground passageway dimly lit by smoking torches bolted to stone walls. There was no sound except the occasional squeak of a rat. No clank of armor sounded from up above. The guard didn't appear to have followed them. "Do you have any idea where we are?"

"I think so, Miss," said Curio. "At least in a general sort of way. We're down near the dungeons. The treasury is one more level down, and I think it's in that direction. I've never been down there, of course. They wouldn't let the likes of me in. But I've heard stories about the treasury being in the same part of the castle as the King's chambers. Far below them, of course. So that would mean it's in the southern corner of the castle, which would be that way."

"Okay," said Nikki. "Well, let's get this over with." She checked to make sure all her hair was still hidden by her page cap. "If we meet any guards you'll have to do the talking. My Realm accent still isn't perfect. Are pages allowed in the dungeons?"

"Yes, Miss," said Curio as they started along the passageway.

"They sometimes bring lunch to the guards, or even to the prisoners. I came down to the dungeons once with Mick. He was handing out loaves of bread to the prisoners and even chatting with some of them. The King is pretty good about following the prison decrees made by his father, about treating prisoners okay. Course, when old Maleficious took over the role of advisor to the King he made some changes. Nasty ones, according to Mick. It was all about longer prison sentences and less food. And I'm guessing that Rufius the Rufian has made things even nastier down here."

After walking a hundred yards or so they came to another passage branching off the main one. Curio stopped and peered down it. He sniffed the air. "Nope, not that way, Miss. I can smell roasting pork. The kitchens is that way. To get to the treasury we need to go through the dungeons, and they're gonna smell much worse than roast pork."

They continued down the main passage. As they went on the floor started to slope down, the air grew colder, and Nikki began to notice a familiar smell. It was the odor of rotten straw mixed with sewage. She remembered it well from the time Maleficious had locked her and Athena in the castle's dungeons. She shivered, remembering all the cockroaches she'd crunched under her feet while pacing in their cell.

Sure enough, they rounded a bend in the passage and a long row of cells appeared on either side of the passage. They looked like tiny caves dug out of the castle's rocky crag. Thick iron bars blocked the entrance to each little cave. Quiet rustling sounds and the occasional cough came from the cells as they passed.

The smell of sewage grew stronger, and Nikki carefully avoided stepping in the rivulet of dirty water which ran down the center of the passageway. The long row of cells didn't look familiar to her. She and Athena must have been locked into a cell in a different part of the dungeons.

They were almost to the end of the row of cells when a tall figure in one of the caves came forward into the light and clutched the iron bars of his cell. The dim torchlight showed him to be very young, barely out of his teens. His youthful face was thinner than it had been back in ImpHaven, but Nikki recognized him immediately.

"Krill!" she gasped.

Krill nodded at her. "Hello, Miss. Hello Curio." His voice was raspy and harsh, as if he was in desperate need of water.

"Oh my gosh!" said Curio, gaping at him. "Mr. Krill!"

"Quiet! Both of you," whispered Nikki, looking up and down the passageway. No guards were in sight, but she could hear faint voices in the distance and a clink of glasses. The guards were probably drinking in the guardroom. Fuzz had managed to rescue her and Athena from the dungeon many months ago by putting valerian root in the guards' ale. It had put them sound asleep. She didn't have any valerian root, but if the guards were drinking heavily enough she wouldn't need it. "Give me the bottle," she whispered to Curio.

Curio nodded and opened the saddlebag. He unwrapped the bottle of acid and handed it carefully to her.

Nikki peered at the lock on Krill's cell door. It was a rusty iron padlock as big as her hand. She set the bottle down on the stone floor and tore off a piece of the linen shirt it had been wrapped in. She carefully un-stoppered the bottle and dipped the linen in the hydrochloric acid. Picking up a stray piece of straw from the floor she skewered the linen with the piece of straw and stuck it deep into the keyhole of the padlock.

A wisp of vinegary smoke came from the keyhole. They all stood staring at the lock for what seemed like hours but was probably only a minute or two.

Nikki was just about to pull out the straw and try adding more acid when the lock suddenly broke into two pieces and fell.

Nikki caught the pieces just before they clattered on the stone floor. She set them down with shaking hands and tried pulling on the door of the cell. At first it didn't budge, but when Krill shoved on it from inside it suddenly opened with a hair-raising creak.

They all froze. The voices from the guardroom up ahead suddenly became louder and somewhere a door banged. The stomp of booted feet echoed along the passage, headed their way.

Krill darted out of the cell, grabbed Nikki by the arm, picked up Curio, and hustled them into the darkness at the back of the little cave.

"The acid!" hissed Nikki.

Krill ran forward, grabbed the saddlebag and the bottle of acid, and carefully shut the cell door.

A wooden sleeping bunk was attached to the stone wall of the cell by iron chains. Krill shooed them underneath it and handed Nikki the saddlebag and the bottle. The bunk creaked as Krill lay down on top of it.

Strange shadows began to play on the walls. Nikki peaked out from under the bunk. Guards with torches were peering into each cell in the row.

"You there!" shouted a guard, banging on the bars of Krill's cell with the hilt of his sword.

Krill lazily sat up on his bunk. "Yeah? What d'you want?"

"What are you doing?" demanded the guard.

"Nothing," said Krill. "Just taking a nap."

The guard lifted his torch and peered into the depths of the cell.

Nikki shrank back into the shadow under the bunk.

"Well, just see that you behave yourself or you'll regret it," said the guard. He and the other guards passed onto the next cell.

Nikki waited until the sound of their boots was very faint before climbing out from under the bunk.

"Good thing they didn't try the door," said Krill, hopping off the bunk.

"Or see the lock," said Curio, pointing at the padlock still lying on the stone floor just outside the cell.

"Yes, we've been lucky," said Nikki. "Now, how are we going to get out of here without the door making that awful sound again?"

"Hang on," said Krill. He rummaged through a pile of garbage shoved against one wall of the cave. "Chicken bone," he said, holding up a gnawed drumstick. "One of the guards isn't such a bad fellow. He gave me this last week. It was left over from his dinner." He cracked the drumstick open and rubbed the greasy marrow on the hinges of the cell door. When he pushed on the door it opened without a sound.

Nikki quickly wrapped the bottle of acid in its linen covering and shoved it into the saddlebag. "Follow Curio," she said to Krill. "We're heading for the treasury."

Krill carefully closed the cell door behind them and they ran as noiselessly as they could down to the end of the row of cells. They passed the guardroom, now empty except for a table littered with empty ale mugs and a chicken carcass.

Curio waved them on and they followed him down a long sloping passageway without cells or side tunnels. The air grew very stuffy. The nearest source of fresh air was a long way away. The passage started to curve in a downward spiral, as if they were walking down a huge stone screw.

"Not much farther," whispered Curio. He adjusted his velvet page cap and brushed some dust off his jacket. "Wait here. They don't usually keep guards stationed this far down, but I'll just go check."

Nikki and Krill sat down with their backs to the stone wall. It was eerily quiet. Even the rats seemed to avoid this part of the castle.

"Have you seen my sister?" whispered Krill. "I haven't seen her since the Knights of the Iron Fist attacked ImpHaven."

"Yes," said Nikki. "I saw Kira here in Cogent Town a few days ago. She was buying food at the market. She disappeared into the crowd before I could talk to her."

"Blast!" said Krill. "She's probably looking for me. I was hoping she'd have the sense to stay on the south coast with Griff and her crew."

"Well, at least she's not been captured," said Nikki. "Not as far as we know. Gwen has. A Lurker grabbed her."

"I'm sorry," said Krill. "How about your friends the imps?"

"Fuzz and Athena are at the Prince's mansion here in Cogent Town," said Nikki. "Athena was injured during the invasion of ImpHaven, but she's healing." She stopped talking suddenly as a shadow loomed up on the curved wall, but it was just Curio.

"All clear," said Curio. "No guards. I hope you're right about that there Devil's Fire, Miss," he said, pointing at the saddlebag hanging from Nikki's shoulder. "Them treasury gates look like a giant fire-breathing dragon couldn't melt them."

When they rounded the last turn of the passage and the treasury gates loomed up in front of them Nikki could see what Curio meant. The gates were two stories tall, with iron bars as thick as the trunk of an oak tree. The stone gatehouse next to them looked like a child's playhouse in comparison. Nikki glanced inside. The gatehouse was empty except for a battered wooden table, a few chairs, and a stone latrine. Nikki held her nose and peered down the latrine. She was surprised to find that she could see all the way down to the ground. A spot of sunlight was shimmering at the end of the stone shaft that the latrine emptied into.

Curio waved her over to the gates. "What do ya think, Miss?" He pointed to a series of massive padlocks holding the gates closed. Each lock was as big as Curio's head.

Nikki bent and peered at the lowest lock. Its huge size was intimidating, but she noticed that the keyhole and the actual mechanism of the lock were quite small. All the extra iron around the keyhole seemed to be mainly for affect. Still, she'd need more acid than she'd used on the lock of Krill's cell. She tried to lift the padlock but it was too heavy.

"Here, Miss," said Krill. "Let me try." With an effort he managed to lift the lock until it was level with the ground.

"Hold it just like that," said Nikki. She quickly opened the saddlebag and unwrapped the bottle of acid. With great care she removed the cork and carefully held the bottle over the padlock. "Move your feet back a bit," she said to Krill. "I don't want any of this dripping on them." When Krill had complied she slowly drizzled the acid into the keyhole of the lock. A slight click came from inside the lock's mechanism. Nikki set the bottle down and re-stoppered it.

They all stood watching and waiting. Nikki nervously drummed her fingers on the gate. Curio did a twitchy little jig. Sweat from Krill's forehead started to drop onto the padlock.

"I'm not sure how much longer I can hold . . ." Krill started to say, when with a loud crack the lock split into two pieces. Nikki just had time to shove the leather saddlebag under it before the pieces crashed to the floor.

They all jumped at the sound, but the saddlebag had mostly muffled it.

"Quick," said Nikki. "Let's do the others."

There were five locks in all and the last one was the trickiest. Krill had to carry the wooden table out of the gatehouse and stand on it to reach the last lock. Nikki climbed up the iron bars of the gate and held on with one hand while pouring the acid into the lock with the other. A tiny drop spilled onto Krill's battered leather boot and ate right through it. Krill hissed in pain but managed to hold onto the lock until it broke. When he climbed down from the table he whipped off his boot. The acid had eaten away the toenail on his big toe.

"Can you walk?" asked Nikki, tearing off a piece of the linen which the acid bottle had been wrapped in.

"Yes," said Krill through gritted teeth. He wiped at his bloody toe with the linen. "Looks like it didn't go all the way through the toe, thank goodness." He wrapped the linen around his foot and pulled his boot back on.

Curio was struggling with the gate. "I think this here bar needs to go up," he said.

Krill limped over, waving Curio out of the way. As he lifted the heavy iron bar the two sides of the tall gate swung open noiselessly. They stepped inside and found a narrow ramp descending into darkness. The light from the smoky torches in the spiral passageway didn't extend this far.

"Kind of awkward," whispered Curio. "How're we gonna know what to steal if we can't see anything?"

"I guess we just take anything that feels like gold," said Nikki. "Or jewels would work too. Anything that's valuable and light enough to carry. We just have to make sure we get enough to satisfy Fortuna."

"Who's Fortuna?" asked Krill.

"The person we're bribing," said Nikki, feeling her way along the wall. "We'll explain if we make it back to the Prince's mansion."

"Ooof!" exclaimed Curio. "Sorry, just tripped over something. I think it's some kind of helmet. Or maybe a shield."

"Leave it," said Nikki. Her foot hit something soft and she

knelt down. "This is more like it," she said. "I think it's a canvas sack. It's jingling. I'll bring it out into the light. See if you can find more sacks." She couldn't lift the sack, but with a great deal of effort she managed to drag it along the floor into the outer passageway. She gave a quick look around, but so far their assault on the castle's treasury hadn't been noticed by the guards. The sack she'd stolen had a thick rope knotted around its mouth. Try as she might Nikki couldn't open it.

Curio came out of the treasury gate dragging another sack, and Krill limped after him carrying a sack under each arm.

"What do you think, Miss?" asked Curio. "We ain't got no way to open 'em, but it sure sounds like they're filled with gold coins."

"I think so too," said Nikki. "I also think we're pushing our luck by staying here any longer. It's time to leave."

"Er, leave how, Miss?" asked Curio. "The guards'll be back in their guardroom by now. We'll have to go right past 'em. And Mr. Krill can't carry four bags of gold all at once."

"He won't have to," said Nikki, dragging a bag of coins towards the gatehouse. "Come on." She dragged the bag inside and stopped next to the latrine.

"Oh, Miss," said Curio, dragging his bag next to hers. "I don't think I like this idea of yours very much." He held his nose and peered into the latrine. "It's a long way down. And there's the smell. Now, me, I've been around pigs in my time. I've mucked out a pig pen or two, so you could say I'm used to smells. But pigs never smelled *this* bad."

"Just hold your breath on the way down," said Nikki.

Krill set his bags down and lifted up the wooden seat of the latrine. "Hmm. It's not a bad plan. Fortunately the shaft doesn't go straight down. Still, it's a pretty steep angle. If we drop all four bags down first you can land on them. They might break your fall a bit."

"*Our* fall, you mean," said Nikki.

Krill shook his head. "I won't fit."

Nikki peered down the latrine again. With a sinking heart she realized that Krill was right. He'd fit into the opening right under the wooden seat, but the long stone shaft that reached to the ground was narrower than the opening. She and Curio would fit, but Krill's broad shoulders were twice as wide as hers. He'd get stuck.

"Not to worry," said Krill, dropping a bag of coins down the shaft. It hit the ground with a soft plop. "I'll find another way out." He dropped the rest of the bags down. "I think my best bet is to hide in the treasury until around midnight. There are fewer guards on duty at night, and the ones stuck with night duty tend to get really drunk. It should be fairly easy to sneak past them. They aren't out hunting for me, remember. They think I'm still locked in my cell."

"I don't know . . ." Nikki said. "Kira will kill me if she finds out I left you here. What if they catch you and lock you up again?"

Krill shrugged. "Then you'll find another way to rescue me." He picked up a squirming Curio and held him over the latrine. "Stop wiggling. And put your arms down by your sides."

Nikki closed her eyes as Krill dropped Curio down the shaft.

A small shriek echoed up the stone shaft as Curio hit the ground, but when Nikki opened her eyes and looked down the shaft he was waving at her from far below.

Nikki gritted her teeth, held her breath, and quickly climbed into the latrine before she lost her nerve. She nodded goodbye to Krill and launched herself into the stone shaft, her arms tightly at her sides, her eyes closed.

Her speed down the shaft was so fast that she didn't really have time to notice the smell, and the landing wasn't as bad as she'd imagined. She landed on her stomach, which knocked the wind out of her, but the bags did help to break her fall. She scrambled to her feet and did a quick check, but all of her bones seemed to be intact.

"Are you okay?" she asked Curio.

"Yes, Miss," he said. "Except for the smell, of course. Baths as a rule aren't my favorite thing, but right now I could take about a dozen of them."

"Baths will have to wait," said Nikki. She peered up the stone shaft. She could just make out the outline of Krill's head far above. She gave him one last wave and then looked around their landing spot. "Do you have any idea where we are?" she asked.

Curio nodded. "I think so, Miss. We're in the middle of the castle's garbage area. Where they dump all the kitchen scraps and other stuff. It's near the main kitchens and the Page House."

"Okay," said Nikki. She picked up her page hat which had fallen off during the trip down the latrine. The hat smelled so bad that she had to suppress the urge to vomit. "I think you might be right about a bath after all," she said. "Our best chance of getting out of the castle is our page uniforms. They make us almost invisible. But they aren't going to keep us from being noticed if we smell like a pig pen." She eyed a nearby mound of garbage. "Help me get the bags over there."

They dragged the bags over to the heap of rotting chicken bones, moldy lettuce leaves, and burnt pieces of wood and covered the bags with the garbage.

"There," said Nikki. "That should keep them safe for now. We'll need to find some kind of cart to transport them down to Cogent Town, but first we need to clean up. Are there baths in the Page House?"

Curio shook his head. "No, Miss. The bath houses are over there, across the square. Next to the stables." He pointed across the flat outcropping of granite which jutted out from the castle's rocky crag like a miniature town square. The kitchens, stables, and the Page House were built on the edge of the flat area. The castle's marble towers and purple flags loomed high above their heads.

Nikki nodded. She held her breath as she put her smelly hat back on and tucked her hair under it. "Let's go."

"Umm, Miss," said Curio as they headed across the square. "There might be a bit of a problem at the baths. I mean, there are men's baths and women's baths. As a page, well, you're supposed to be a boy. The bath attendant will expect you to go into the men's baths."

"Oh," said Nikki, slowing to a halt. She glanced around the buildings surrounding the square while she tried to decide what to do. The stables caught her eye. "What about the horse troughs? Maybe we could just dunk ourselves in those."

"I don't think that's going to work, Miss," said Curio, pointing to the dark brown streaks covering the back of his page uniform. "What we need is soap, hot water, and some hard scrubbing . . ." He paused suddenly, staring over at the kitchens. "I have an idea, Miss. You go over there and hide in that shadowy area between those two buildings. I'll be right back."

Before Nikki had a chance to respond Curio darted off toward the bath houses. A man pushing a wheelbarrow full of cabbages was headed in her direction, so she quickly walked over to the kitchens and tried to casually melt into the shadows. The smell of baking bread wafted through the air. It would have been more enticing if her own smell wasn't so strong. She pinched her nose shut and tried not to think about what she was covered in. Fortunately Curio wasn't gone long.

"Got them, Miss," he said, running up to her waving a scrub brush and a big bar of soap. "Now, that building behind us is where they make the tea for all the workers down here. Pages, stable boys, and kitchen helpers go through so many cups of tea every day you wouldn't believe it. Anyway, they always has big kettles full of water boiling away all day long. All we gotta do is snatch one and grab a couple of roasting pans and we'll be all set."

The snatching and grabbing were harder than Curio had made it out to be, but by biding their time until the tea area of the kitchen was empty they managed to haul one of the large kettles outside. They plunked it down in an isolated corner behind a cart piled high with turnips.

Curio took off his page jacket, dumped it in a roasting pan, and poured hot water on it. "It's working already, Miss," he said, pointing at the water in the pan as it turned dark brown. "Just a bit of scrubbing and we'll be all set."

Nikki took off her jacket. One of the maids at the Prince's mansion had washed her underwear and her Westlake Debate Team t-shirt and she had those on underneath her page uniform. Fortunately the t-shirt went almost to her knees. She took off her purple velvet trousers and carefully averted her eyes as Curio did the same.

After using up all the hot water and doing some heavy scrubbing they both pulled their soggy but clean uniforms back on.

"Aren't people going to stare at us because we're all wet?" asked Nikki, stuffing her hair under her dripping hat.

"No need to worry about that, Miss," said Curio. "Pages sometimes help give the King's hunting dogs a bath. You get a right soaking doing that. As long as we don't go into the fancy ballrooms and council chambers at the top of the castle and drip all over the floors no one will care."

"They might care about two pages stealing kettles out of the kitchens," a voice suddenly said behind them.

Nikki and Curio whirled around.

"Mick!" said Curio. "Didn't see ya there."

"I know ya didn't, mate," said the tall page, leaning casually against the turnip wagon. "Odd place for you and yer friend to have a bath."

"Well, you know how it is," said Curio. "There's no privacy in them there bath houses, and me friend he's shy."

Mick snorted. He darted forward and whisked off Nikki's cap. Her long dark hair tumbled down.

"Who you think yer fooling, little Curio?" said Mick. "I knowed yer friend was a girl the moment I met her. And what's more, I know who she is. Some of them wanted posters in town are very life-like."

Curio's thin little face hardened. "What do you want, Mick?"

Mick grinned and rubbed his fingers together.

"We ain't got no money, Mick," said Curio.

"Bet ya could scrounge some up if ya really tried," said Mick. "Course, I could always just go see the captain of the guards. There's a nice fat reward out fer you two."

"Can I talk to you for a minute?" said Nikki, pulling Curio away out of Mick's earshot. "Let's just give him a few coins from the bags."

Curio shook his head. "Nah, a few coins won't be enough fer him. Mick's greedy, he is."

"Well, then let's give him a lot of coins," said Nikki.

"No, Miss," said Curio. "Mick's not above bashing us on the head and just stealing all the bags. I got a better idea." He walked back to Mick.

"You two done with yer little conference?" asked Mick. "I got places to be."

"You ever heard of the Prince of Physics, Mick?" asked Curio.

Mick raised an eyebrow. "Course I have. Everyone in the Realm's heard of him. What's he got to do with anything?"

"Well," said Curio. "It just so happens that he's a good friend of ours. If you help us get back into Cogent Town and don't rat us out to the captain of the guards, the Prince will see that you get a pile of gold. More than you can spend in a whole year. Plus he might even introduce you to the King."

Nikki glanced uncertainly at Mick. She thought Curio was laying it on a bit thick. To her surprise Mick didn't laugh in Curio's face.

"Yeah, I heard something about that," said Mick, giving Nikki a searching look. "I heard rumors that she's friends with imps and it's well-known that the Prince is an imp-lover. I even heard rumors that she's been inside the Prince's estate down in Kingston. Useful guy to have on yer side, the Prince. Tell ya what, little Curio. You introduce me to the Prince and I won't rat on you and yer friend."

"Deal," said Curio. "Now, you got any ideas about how to sneak us back into town?"

Mick grinned nastily. "Oh, I has a very nice idea."

Chapter Five

Payoff

NIKKI POKED HER head out from under a pile of wilted lettuce leaves and peered over the edge of the garbage wagon. They had reached the end of the long, steep road which led down from the castle. The wagon was clattering over the cobblestones of Cogent Town's main street. Mick was whistling a tune from up on the driver's seat.

"We're almost there," Nikki whispered to Curio, who was throwing up in a corner under a pile of torn burlap sacks and potato peels.

Curio just groaned in response.

Nikki had been able to avoid upchucking by keeping her nose firmly pinched shut during their entire ride down from the castle. She lay back down again and covered herself with lettuce leaves, rotting chicken bones and pumpkin rinds. She could feel one of the bags of coins against her feet. She and Curio had managed to drag the bags into the wagon and hide them under the garbage while Mick was busy hitching up the horses.

The wagon swerved sharply around a corner and came to a sudden halt.

Mick knocked on the side of the wagon. "Everybody out."

Nikki and Curio climbed out, leaving the bags of coins under the garbage.

"Where are we?" asked Curio, wiping his mouth on his sleeve.

"In an alley," said Mick. "Just up the street from the Prince's mansion." He motioned them to follow him.

When Mick's back was turned Nikki snatched Curio's page cap off his head and threw it into the back of the wagon.

"What did ya do that for, Miss?" asked Curio. "I need that fer me disguise."

"I know," whispered Nikki. "It'll give us a reason to come back here to collect the bags."

"Oh, good thinking, Miss," said Curio.

They followed Mick down the street to the tall main gate belonging to the Prince's house. Nikki glanced sharply around for any sign that Rounders or Lurkers were watching the house, but she didn't spot anything out of the ordinary. A street sweeper was lazily pushing his broom along the pavement, and a well-dressed woman was walking a tiny poodle, but otherwise the street was empty.

Mick knocked on the gate and stepped aside. He shoved Nikki in front of him.

The gate swung open and a tall, spear-carrying guard frowned down at them. "Yes?" he said, glancing at their page uniforms.

"Um," said Nikki. "We have a message for the Prince."

The guard raised an eyebrow. "And it took all three of you to deliver it?"

"It's a special message," said Nikki.

The guard snorted, but grudgingly moved back and waved them through the gate. "Wait here," he said. "I'll send for Morton."

They waited awkwardly in front of the house while two footmen in black livery lined with silver thread eyed them suspiciously. Finally Morton, the Prince's Head Butler, appeared and descended the front steps of the house. He brushed a speck of dust off of his green satin tailcoat and strode up to them.

"Now, what's all this about a special . . ." He broke off, his eyes narrowing as he recognized Nikki and Curio. "What . . . ?"

"Um, this is our friend Mick," said Nikki hurriedly. "He's always wanted to have a look inside the Prince's mansion. I know it's a bother, but if you could let him have just a quick peek that would be really nice of you. He's a senior page in very good standing. Never had any complaints filed about him from up at the castle."

"I don't think . . ." Morton began.

"Also, Curio and I need to borrow this for a minute. We'll bring it right back." Before anyone could object Nikki darted over to a wheelbarrow she'd spotted in the garden next to a massive hydrangea bush. She trundled it across the lawn and out of the open gate before anyone could react.

"Forgot me hat!" Curio yelled at a confused Morton as he ran to catch up with Nikki.

"Anybody following us?" asked Nikki as she raced along the street pushing the wheelbarrow.

"Not yet, Miss," said Curio. "That guard is poking his head out of the gate, but it don't look like he's set to chase us. He just looks kinda befuddled. Like a sheep that just got hit on the head with a hammer. I guess it's not every day that someone steals the Prince's wheelbarrow."

Nikki nodded. "I think we can pull this off if no one comes looking for us." She made a sharp turn into the alley where the garbage wagon was parked. It was still there, and no one was in the alley. "Quick, get your hat and help me with the bags."

It was easier dragging the bags out of the wagon than into it.

They covered them with garbage and Nikki slowly trundled the wheelbarrow back to the Prince's mansion. The gate was still open.

"Check and see if Mick's gone into the house," she whispered to Curio.

Curio poked his head around the side of the gate. "All clear," he said, waving her forward. "That guard is still there. He glared at me awfully fierce-like, but Mick's nowhere in sight."

Nikki shoved the wheelbarrow through the gate. Ignoring the shouts of the guard she pushed it across the lawn and dumped it straight into the huge hydrangea bush next to the front steps. The bush was in full bloom and its heavy blue flowers and thick leaves hid the bags of coins completely. Nikki parked the wheelbarrow in front of the bush and wiped her grimy hands on her page jacket. "All done," she said, smiling sweetly at the guard. "Just a little present from the chief gardener up at the castle. Some special fertilizer to make the Prince's hydrangea's extra-blue."

Before the guard could respond they ran past the footmen and up the front steps of the mansion and knocked on the door. It opened immediately to reveal an angry Morton glaring down at them.

"Senior page," he huffed. "That boy is nothing but a common street hooligan or I'll eat my shoes. How he ever landed a job as a page is beyond me. I have two footmen watching him like a hawk to make sure he doesn't steal the silverware."

"We're sorry," said Nikki. "But we had no choice. We had to get out of the castle in a hurry and Mick offered to help us if we'd introduce him to the Prince."

Morton's eyebrows rose. "Introduce him to the Prince! Certainly not. He's lucky I haven't thrown him out onto the street headfirst."

"You can't do that," said Nikki. "He knows too much about

us. We have to keep him happy or he'll run straight to Rufius. You'll have the castle guards surrounding the house in no time. And speaking of keeping him happy, can you ask a couple of footmen to carry in some bags for us? They're in the hydrangea bush."

"We got what we was sent up to the castle fer," said Curio, standing up ramrod straight and looking very proud.

Morton gave them a baffled look, but finally nodded and went out the front door. They could hear him giving orders to the footmen. A few minutes later he re-appeared leading the footmen. Each one was carrying two bags of coins.

"Bring them into the library," said Morton. "Then resume your post. And make sure that the guard has closed and locked the front gate. We don't want any more unwelcome visitors."

It stung a little, being lumped in with unwelcome visitors, but Nikki ignored the comment and followed the footmen into the library. They dumped the bags on top of a rosewood desk and left. Curio closed the door after them.

Nikki rooted around in the drawers of the desk. "This should do," she said, holding up a sharp-looking letter opener. She sawed at the rope holding one of the bags closed until it suddenly split open with a snap. The mouth of the bag opened wide and Nikki stuck her hand inside. When she pulled it out it was filled with golden coins sparkling in the light from the windows.

Curio stared at her hand, his eyes wide. "Gosh and pull me ears, Miss. That is a sight to see. We must have enough coins in them bags to buy a whole estate, just like the Prince has in Kingston."

Nikki dropped the coins back into the bag. "Well, I don't know about that, but let's hope we have enough to bribe Fortuna. And Mick also. Fuzz and Athena will know how much it'll take to make Fortuna happy, but what about Mick? You've known him for years. How many coins should we give him?"

Curio plucked one of the coins out of the bag and rubbed it thoughtfully between his fingers. "I'd say about two handfuls, Miss. That'd be more money than a page would make in maybe ten years. But we might also have to introduce Mick to the Prince like we said we would. He's a social climber, Mick is. He likes to rub elbows with powerful types. Wouldn't be surprised if he makes it all the way to courtier someday." He suddenly frowned and peered closely at the coin he was holding. "What . . .?" He put the coin down on the desk and scratched at it with the point of the letter opener. A small scrap of gold peeled off the coin and fluttered to the floor.

Nikki snatched the scrap off the floor. It crumpled in her fingers. "This is gold leaf!" she cried. She dug into the bag and pulled out a handful of coins. She dumped them on the desk and scratched at them with the letter opener. The gold peeled away from all of them.

"Oh, Miss. This is not good," said Curio. "All that effort and all we gets is fake coins. D'you think they're all like this?"

Nikki handed him the letter opener. "Open the other bags," she said. She sat down at the desk and stared at the peeling coin in her hand. A faint film of white powder was visible under the gold leaf. Her heart sank as she realized what it was. Just to make sure she put the coin down on the desk and picked up a heavy brass table lamp. She smashed the lamp down on the coin. When she picked the coin up again it was much flatter. "Lead," she said. "The coins are lead covered with gold leaf. They're almost worthless." She wiped her fingers carefully on the green felt runner covering the desk. The white powder was lead oxide, which was toxic. Such a tiny amount probably wouldn't hurt her, but she made a mental note to wash her hands carefully before her next meal.

"Here's a coin from each of the other bags, Miss," said Curio, placing three coins on the desk.

Nikki smashed the brass lamp down on each one. Two of them flattened like a pancake, but the third made a ringing sound when it was hit and looked un-squashed. Nikki scratched at it with the letter opener. The gilt still peeled off, but instead of a dull grey metal covered in white powder there was a black-looking substance. Nikki scratched at the black and it flaked off, revealing a shiny metal. "Silver," she said. "It's silver covered in gold leaf. Not as valuable as solid gold, but a lot better than gilt-covered lead."

Curio leaned over the desk for a better look. "What's that black stuff, Miss?"

"Tarnish," said Nikki. "Hydrogen sulfide in the air tarnishes silver. Makes it turn black. It's kind of like the way iron rusts, though that's called oxidation and it's not quite the same thing." She flipped the coin over and peered at the back. It was stamped with a picture of someone in profile. She held the coin out to Curio. "Who's picture is that?" she asked.

"That's the old King," said Curio. "Our King's father. He's on all the coins. Well, on all the gold ones. That's how you know they're real gold. The silver coins are stamped with a picture of Castle Cogent, and the copper ones have a picture of the Southern Castle." He frowned. "Someone could get into a lot of trouble making fake coins like this. Specially coins stamped with the official portrait. That's treason, that is. It could cause real trouble by making folks not trust the currency of the Realm. Also it would be real hard to do. The stamps for the coins are in the royal mint, up at the castle, and they have lots of guards watching them day and night. I think they have more guards in the mint than they do in the treasury. I guess the King thinks it's more of a crime to make your own money than it is to steal his."

"Who would have access to the royal mint?" asked Nikki.

"Well, the King, of course," said Curio. "I doubt he ever goes there, but he could if he wanted to. And Mr. Geber, cause he's the royal alchemist now that old Maleficious is dead. He'd help with the mixing of metals for the coins. The gold coins ain't one-hundred percent gold, of course. Cause gold's too soft. They mix in a bit of some other metal. Not sure which. Maybe copper."

"And Rufius," said Nikki. "He would have access. The King's new right-hand man."

Curio stared at her unhappily. "Yes, Miss. It's pretty likely that Rufius the Ruffian has had these here fake coins made."

"It wouldn't surprise me if Geber helped him," said Nikki. "I spent a bit of time with Geber in his workshop down in D-ville. He's not a very nice person. Not very ethical. He's maybe not quite as bad as Rufius, not as power-hungry. But I don't think it would take much to persuade Geber to make fake coins. Especially if he got to keep some of the profits."

"They must be hiding all the gold somewhere," said Curio. "All the gold what should have gone into coin-making. I wonder how many of the gold coins in the treasury are fake. They could bankrupt the Realm if they keep this up."

"Yes," said Nikki. "We need to tell Fuzz and Athena about this. And the Prince too. But it'll have to wait. Right now we've got to solve the Fortuna problem." She got up from the desk and stood staring down at the bags of coins on the floor. "So, we've got only one bag of silver. Somehow I don't think that's going to be enough to satisfy Fortuna." She tipped the bag containing the gilt-covered silver coins on its side and a flood of coins spilled onto the parquet floor. Most of them shone bright and golden, but a handful had visible chips where the silver peeked through. Nikki glanced around the richly furnished library. Row after row of leather-bound books stared back at her. A few of the books had gilt letters on their covers, but that wasn't enough gold for her purpose. An oil-painting near the window caught her eye. It was a pretty scene of a summer meadow filled with daisies, but it wasn't the picture she was looking at. It was the frame. She snatched the letter opener from the desk and applied its sharp point to the picture frame. A long peel of gilt fell off and floated to the floor. Nikki picked it up and went over to the pile of coins. She chose one where the gilt had chipped off. The gold leaf from the picture frame was very soft and she soon had the chip on the coin entirely covered. She held it up to Curio. "What do you think? It looks like a real gold coin. If we fix all the chips and scratches we might be able to fool Fortuna."

Curio took the coin. "Maybe, Miss," he said. "Course, she'll do the old tooth test. She'll bite a few coins. So we can't use the lead ones. Lead is soft enough to bite."

"Okay," said Nikki. "So we'll just patch up the coins in the silver bag. We'll have to hope that one bag will be enough."

Chapter Six

The Deadly Plan

N IKKI NERVOUSLY CLENCHED and unclenched her fists, watching as Fortuna dipped her be-ringed hand into the bag of coins. The old fortune teller peered at the coins in her palm suspiciously, while Fuzz, Athena, and Curio held their breath.

They were all seated in armchairs around the fireplace in the parlor. Night had fallen and the banked fire threw out serpent-shaped shadows that reached out to draw them all into the embers.

Nikki watched the firelight shine through Fortuna's beaded necklaces. It suddenly occurred to her that the old fortune-teller looked shabbier than the last time she'd seen her. In Deception-ville she'd been wearing jeweled cloaks and fancy gowns. Now she was back to wearing the ragged shawls she'd had on when Nikki had first met her on the Isle of Ignorance. It looked like Fortuna's determination to follow a path toward wealth had taken a wrong turn.

As Curio had predicted, Fortuna bit down hard on several coins. Then she dumped the whole bag onto the carpet in front of the fire and carefully counted them.

"Three hundred stamped gold coins," she said, plopping back

down on a padded footstool. "Not bad. Not bad at all." She snapped her fingers at Curio. "Put them back in the bag, boy. And see that you don't palm any. I'm watching you."

Curio kneeled on the carpet and carefully put all the coins back in the bag.

"Well?" said Fuzz impatiently. "Do we have a deal or not? Are you going to finally tell us what you know?"

Fortuna just smirked at him. "I'm feeling a bit peckish. Send for one of the footmen. Tell him to bring a tray of pastries and a pot of strong black tea. And plenty of sugar."

Athena stared at her stone-faced from the armchair closest to the fire. "I do not think she knows anything, this palm reader and seller of worthless potions. I say we throw her out of this house with no gold and no pastries. There are other ways to find out what Rufius and his followers are up to."

"Hold your tongue, imp," spat Fortuna. "I have powerful friends up at the castle. And in D-ville also. You would do well not to cross me."

"But do you?" asked Fuzz. "Have powerful friends? We've seen you with Avaricious, the wealthy D-ville merchant. And we know that you once met with Rufius in the D-ville town hall when you were selling your quack potions to gullible nobles. But my guess is that your fortunes have fallen since then. Your powerful friends have deserted you. Otherwise why would you be here, trying to sell information?"

Fortuna's face twisted and she flashed Fuzz a look of hatred.

They all sat quietly watching her as she seemed to battle with herself.

Finally she spoke. "Promise me safe passage to anywhere I wish to go in Cogent Town, and a footman to carry the bag of coins, and I'll tell you what I know."

Fuzz glanced at Athena. She nodded.

"Speak," said Fuzz.

Fortuna cleared her throat and pulled her multi-colored shawls tighter around her shoulders. "The dam," she said. "The dam on the Clearwater River. Cogent Town's pride and joy. Built centuries ago to provide clean drinking water to the city. Without it the city would be only a tenth the size it is now. Its wells would dry up and its fields could not be irrigated."

"Yes," said Fuzz, waving his hand impatiently. "We're well aware of Clearwater Dam. What about it?"

"Flood," hissed Fortuna. "A flood so huge and unstoppable that nothing will be left of the city. Not this house, not the Fox and Fig, not the houses of the nobles nor the houses of the poor. The castle on its high crag would likely survive, but nothing else."

"Nonsense," said Fuzz. "Clearwater Dam is unbreakable. Impossible to damage, even slightly. It has stood for hundreds of years and there is not a single crack in it. I expect Rufius knows this perfectly well. He's just fed you a rumor, to spread fear and confusion. We aren't going to pay you three hundred gold coins just to whisper nonsense into our ears."

"The black powder," said Fortuna quietly, a cruel smile on her face.

Nikki flinched, her fists clenching so tightly that her fingernails cut into her palms. Gwen's gunpowder. That was what Rufius wanted Gwen for. To make enough gunpowder to blow up a dam.

Fuzz looked confused for a second, but then Nikki could see a memory cross his face. He and Athena had been at the Southern Castle when Gwen had escaped from its dungeons. She'd blown a hole in its walls using gunpowder.

"Miss Gwendolyn," said Athena in a shaking voice. "She knows how to make this powder."

Fortuna nodded. "Yes. That old fool Geber has her notes.

The Lurkers stole them from her rooms in D-ville. But Geber hasn't been able to make head nor tail of them. Apparently they're written in some kind of code. Maybe Geber was competent in his youth, I don't know. Personally I think he was always just a blowhard. But now he's worthless. Even if he could read the notes I doubt he'd be able to make the powder. That's why they took the girl. Snatched her at the Fox and Fig a day ago. She'll make the black powder for them. As much as they need."

"No she won't," said Nikki, glaring at Fortuna. "They can't make her."

"Oh but they can," said Fortuna, smiling with her crooked teeth and her dead eyes. "She'll make it for them in the end." She lurched up from the padded footstool, her long grey hair tangling in her clattering necklaces. "Now, if you'll call a footman to carry my gold I think I'll be going. I don't want to overstay my welcome." She left the parlor, quietly laughing.

Nikki, Fuzz, and Athena sat staring at each other in shock. They didn't notice that Curio had followed Fortuna out of the room until he returned a few minutes later.

"I just wanted to make sure she left," he said, plopping down on the carpet in front of the fire and hugging his knees to his chest. "She's the kind who'll try to steal the family silver on the way out. But old Morton the butler was watching her like a hawk. Speaking of Morton, he's still got Mick squirreled away in the kitchen. Mick's eating his way through a whole roast chicken. Seems like a bad idea to keep him here. Fortuna's not the only one who'll try a spot of silver stealing."

Fuzz waved an impatient hand. "We've got bigger problems than one light-fingered page." He glanced at Athena, who was staring into the fire. "Any ideas, old girl?" he asked.

Athena shook herself and sat up straight, the customary sternness returning to her face. "We need to get this information about Clearwater Dam to his Highness immediately," she said. "He will know what to do."

Fuzz and Nikki exchanged glances.

Nikki knew exactly what he was thinking. Athena was still placing too much confidence in the King. The same King who had turned over so much of his power to Rufius, because he was too lazy to be bothered with the hard work of ruling the Realm.

"I don't think we should do that," Fuzz said quietly. "Rufius is so close to the King now that anything we tell his Highness will become known by him."

Athena looked so shocked by this that she sat opening and closing her mouth, but no sound came out.

"I agree," Nikki said quickly. "We should tell the Prince and Bertie. They'll know whether it's a good idea to tell the King. Or not to tell him."

Athena stared at her with such an appalled look that Nikki turned beet red.

"The two of you cannot possibly be suggesting that we should withhold vital information from the rightful ruler of the Realm?" Athena asked, her tiny hands clutching the arms of her chair. "We are the King's emissaries. Our first duty is to him."

"Our first duty is to the Realm," said Fuzz. "And to its citizens. The King is only one person. Thousands of people will die if Clearwater Dam is destroyed. Our first priority is to stop that from happening."

Nikki watched a tortured mix of emotions pass across Athena's face. She felt sorry for the imp, but she also realized something she hadn't before. Athena was a monarchist. Her loyalty was to the royal family of the Realm. That didn't make her a bad person, but it put her somewhat in opposition to Fuzz, and to Nikki herself for that matter. Nikki had up to that point just accepted that the Realm was a monarchy. She hadn't really thought about it all that much. Events had moved so quickly during her time in the Realm of Reason that she hadn't had time to mull over the Realm's political system. She was used to the democratic system in her home state of Wisconsin, and in the United States. Back home people were elected by voters, they didn't inherit political office from their family. But because the Realm was so many centuries behind her own modern world in terms of technology she'd just assumed that monarchy was its natural state.

"I agree that our main goal is to stop any sabotage to the dam," said Athena finally, breaking into Nikki's thoughts. "But the best way to proceed is to tell the King everything we know."

Fuzz was about to respond when the parlor door was flung open and four people rushed into the room.

"I apologize madam," gasped Morton, the Prince's butler, to Athena. His neatly oiled hair was falling into his eyes and his green satin tailcoat was torn in several places. "These people burst through the back door and knocked down two footmen who tried to stop them. Why the guards let them through the front gate is a mystery. I will most definitely get to the bottom of it. When I find the guard responsible he will be fired at once."

"We didn't come through the gate," said a deep voice. It was Darius. The stonemason who Gwen was in love with, who'd helped them rescue the imps imprisoned in the Southern Castle, and who Nikki and Curio had seen drinking with Rufius in the Fox and Fig tavern only a day ago.

"We came over the wall." It was Krill. He stood towering over Morton, who was trying in vain to pull him out of the room.

"We climbed an apple tree in the back yard of the mansion next door. It was growing over the Prince's wall." It was Kira, her braids askew and her sailor's tunic and leggings torn and dirty.

"Kira!" gasped Nikki, jumping up. She hugged her friend,

tears in her eyes. "You look awful!" She gently pushed Kira down into the armchair she'd been sitting in. "Morton, can we have some food brought in? These are friends of ours. I'm sure they're hungry."

Morton looked inclined to argue, but Fuzz and Athena both nodded at him and he huffily left the room.

Kira leaned wearily back into the armchair and Krill stepped in front of the fire to warm himself. He was still limping slightly from his injury up at the castle.

"Um, Miss," said Curio to Kira, "your hair seems to be moving. It might be a rat. Don't move, I'll whack it with a poker." He stretched out an arm to grab the fire tongs.

"It's not a rat," said Kira hastily, waving at Curio to put down the tongs. She reached under her thick braids and pulled out a very bedraggled kitten.

"Cation!" exclaimed Nikki.

"Yes," said Kira, handing her over to Nikki. "She was hunting mice in the dungeons up at the castle. I spotted her when we were looking for a way out. I recognized her as your kitten right away. She has that funny-shaped spot on her nose."

Nikki cradled the purring kitten. "I swear she's grown since I last saw her, which wasn't that long ago. Me and Curio were up in the castle, undercover as pages. Cation was running around the rooms of Carmela, the King's housekeeper. I left her there because she seemed well-fed and happy, and me and Curio were kind of on the run."

"Well, maybe you could leave her here," said Kira, looking around the richly-furnished parlor. "She'd probably eat better than the rest of us. I've never been in the King's quarters up at the castle, but this looks just about as fancy as anything the King might have."

"How's your friend Rufius?" Fuzz asked suddenly, staring

hard at Darius as he paced back and forth behind them, just outside the firelight.

Darius flinched but didn't respond.

"You two looked awfully chummy in the Fox and Fig," continued Fuzz. "Regular drinking buddies, you were. So, are you part of his inner circle now? His loyal servant?"

Darius took a step toward Fuzz, his face dark with anger.

Krill quickly stepped between Darius and the imp. "Move back," he said coldly. "*Now.*"

Darius stared at him for a long moment, then shrugged and sat down in a chair against the wall.

"Why are you here?" Nikki asked him as Cation purred in her ear. "I thought you were, what's the name for it? A Returner?"

"A Remover," said Athena quietly.

"Yeah, a Remover," said Nikki. "You want all the imps removed from the Realm. Which is awful and completely ridiculous. They have just as much right to be here as you do."

Darius just sat with his arms crossed, staring silently at the floor.

"He's here because of Gwen," said Kira. "He knows Rufius has her. We think she's being held somewhere in the castle dungeons. We tried to find her when I was rescuing Krill."

Krill rolled his eyes. "You didn't rescue me you little nincompoop. I'd almost found a way out of the dungeons when you came along and got me spotted by the castle guards."

Kira snorted. "This is the thanks I get for trying to help my twin brother. My baby brother."

Krill threw up his hands. "I'm only an hour younger than you. Stop trying to mother me."

"I wouldn't need to if you had an ounce of common sense," said Kira.

"Stop, just stop," said Fuzz, waving at them to be quiet. "We don't have time for family squabbles." He turned back to Darius. "If you're so concerned about Gwen then why aren't you up at the castle trying to rescue her? Surely your connection to Rufius should come in handy."

Darius shook his head. "I tried. Rufius wouldn't listen. He wants Gwen to do something. To make something for him. I don't know what it is. He wouldn't tell me."

"We know what it is," said Athena quietly. "But this does not explain why you are here, in this house. Why would a Remover come seeking help from imps?"

"Because of the Mystic Men," said Darius, not looking at Athena. "That's what Rufius calls them. They're a large group of men from the Mystic Mountains. They're up at the castle, staying in one of the guard barracks. They number more than a hundred and many of them are armed and warlike. They're angry over the death of Maleficious, who they seem to almost worship. I'm not quite sure why. Something to do with some land deep in the Mystic Mountains that he granted them. I think Maleficious used to have family in that area of the Realm. Rufius has been feeding these men lies about imps being the ones who murdered Maleficious. He's also told them lies about certain noble families here in Cogent Town. He claims certain nobles are plotting with the imps to overthrow the King. The Mystic Men are very volatile. They're a danger to more than just the imps. I thought they bore watching, so I took it upon myself to befriend some of them. I drank with them in their barracks at night, and played cards with them. I listened to their conversations. And that is why I am here. Because of something I overheard. They are plotting to attack certain areas of Cogent Town. To set fire to the homes of imps and the homes of nobles they think are in league with the imps. If they are not stopped many people will be killed and Cogent Town will be set ablaze."

"So are you here in this house because you think the Prince can stop this plot, or because you think this house is a target of these Mystic Men?" asked Fuzz.

"Both," said Darius, still staring at the carpet.

Fuzz raised an inquiring eyebrow at Athena.

"We will let you tell your information to the Prince," said Athena. "Despite the obvious mistrust we imps have of Removers, if your story is true then the danger is too great to keep this to ourselves. The imps and nobles who are targets must be warned."

"Where *is* the Prince?" asked Nikki. "I haven't seen him all day. Bertie's not around either."

"They are out visiting certain noble houses in town," said Athena. "They are trying to put together a resistance. Nobles who will stand up to Rufius and remove him from his position as advisor to the King. This will be very difficult, of course. Rufius has not only the Knights of the Iron Fist on his side, but now also these Mystic Men. And who knows how many of the castle guards he has bribed."

"These nobles the Prince is talking to," said Nikki, "isn't it likely that they're the same ones that the Mystic Men are targeting?"

"Probably," said Fuzz. "It's well known around town that the nobles have split into two camps. Those who oppose Rufius and want him kicked out of Castle Cogent, and those who are friendly to him. Probably because he's bribed them. Or because he's played on their anti-imp prejudices. Quite a few nobles are Removers."

Nikki nodded, staring down at the carpet, lost in thought. She'd had an idea, but it was risky and she had a feeling that Fuzz and Athena would try to talk her out of it.

At that moment Morton came back into the room, leading several footmen carrying silver trays piled high with bread, cheese, and grapes. They set up a low table in front of the fire and put the food down on it. Krill and Kira dug in eagerly, and even Darius came out from the shadows and selected a piece of cheese and a glass of wine. Cation leaped down from Nikki's shoulder and launched herself at a tray. She dragged a piece of cheese off it and carried it in front of the fire where she curled up on the rug and alternated between purring and dainty nibbling.

Nikki saw her chance. While everyone was focused on the food she quietly got up and slipped out of the room. She hurried to the front of the house and snatched up her page hat from a hat rack near the front door. She carefully tucked her hair under the hat and slipped outside. There were two footmen standing on either side of the door, but they ignored her. The spear-carrying guard at the front gate just shrugged at her request to open the gate and instead let her out through a small side door built into the wall.

Nikki hesitated in the shadow of the wall surrounding the Prince's mansion. The night was cloudy, with no moon, and the street was very dark. She peered into the darkness and listened carefully. She was pretty sure that people were watching the mansion, but in her purple page uniform she was nearly invisible if she kept to the shadows. Keeping close to the wall she headed in what she thought was the right direction.

Chapter Seven

Allies

“BUT I DON'T understand what Gwen has to do with any of this,” said Lady Ursula, absentmindedly petting the tiny poodle in her lap. The poodle wore a pink bow which matched Lady Ursula's pink satin ball gown. Nikki had caught Gwen's mother just as she came down the steps of the mansion of the Duchess of Falsa. Lady Ursula and the Duchess had been on their way to a ball and they had not been happy to have a page interrupt their night out. After much pleading Lady Ursula had finally agreed to give Nikki a moment of her time. The Duchess had departed for the ball in her carriage while Nikki and Gwen's mother went into the mansion's front parlor.

“Gwen has special skills and knowledge,” Nikki said for the third time. “You remember what her basement laboratory in Muddled Manor was like. All those chemicals and potions. That kind of knowledge makes her valuable to Rufius.”

“Such a dear boy,” said Lady Ursula. “He was very complimentary about our rose garden at the Manor. I feel no embarrassment in saying that a great deal of our success with the roses is due to me. I keep careful watch over our gardeners and instruct them on how much to water the rose bushes. Red roses need more water than white ones, you know.”

Nikki sighed. "Yes, your rose garden was lovely. But right now we need to focus on Gwen. She's in real danger. We think she's somewhere in Castle Cogent. Possibly in the dungeons. We need your help to get her out."

Lady Ursula patted her white hair with a gloved hand. "Don't be silly, child. Gwen isn't in any dungeon. The very idea. She's a noble of the highest rank. No one would ever dream of putting her in a dungeon. The King wouldn't stand for it."

"I doubt that the King knows," said Nikki.

"Nonsense," said Lady Ursula firmly. "Rufius is the King's right-hand man. Anything Rufius knows the King knows as well. Now, I think we've wasted enough time on this. I need to get to the ball. Lady Hyacinth is holding a card tournament after the dancing. I've been practicing all day with my maid and I just *know* I'm going to win first prize." She set the poodle down on the floor and rose from her chair. "If you'll excuse me I need to find the butler. He'll need to order a hired carriage since the Duchess has gone off without me. You can show yourself out."

Nikki darted in front of her before she could leave the room. "Please, Lady Ursula. It's not just Gwen who's in danger. There's a plot to burn down many homes in Cogent Town, including homes of the nobility. You wouldn't want any friends of yours to lose their homes, would you?"

Lady Ursula waved an airy hand. "More nonsense. Where *do* you get these stories, my dear? You're positively brimming with drama. You should consider writing plays for the King's theater up at the castle. I'm sure they'd be very popular. Now please get out of my way."

Nikki watched helplessly as Lady Ursula left the room. She'd counted on Gwen's mother being concerned for her daughter's safety, but she'd forgotten how divorced from reality she could be. She was about to leave when a figure appeared in the doorway. It was a young woman dressed in the neat black dress and pale blue apron worn by a lady's maid.

"Hello, Miss," the maid said quietly. "My name is Ava. I was listening at the door. Yes, I freely admit it. Maybe it is not such a nice habit, but the life of a servant is frequently boring and we all must find amusement where we can. Please, sit down." She sat down in the chair vacated by Lady Ursula and waved Nikki to the chair next to her.

"Um, okay," said Nikki, eyeing her nervously as she sat down.

The maid smiled. "Do not worry. I am not here to announce to the household that you are not what you appear. Your page costume is clever, but when you speak it is easy to tell that you are a young girl." She paused for a moment as if listening for noises in the house. The smile left her face. "I heard what you said to Lady Ursula about her daughter. I believe you, even if her ladyship did not. I know several people who work up at the castle. They have heard very unpleasant things about this young man called Rufius. I am very sorry about Miss Gwen, but I cannot do anything to help her. But the other thing, the fires you mentioned. There I might be of some use."

"Really?" asked Nikki in surprise.

"Yes," said the maid. "The nobility, they have of course their own social circle. They trade gossip and rumors and even sometimes they pass along useful knowledge to each other. And their servants do these things as well. We have our own social circle. All the maids and butlers and footmen and grooms who work for the nobility. I have a sister who works as a maid in the household of Lady Hyacinth, the mansion which Lady Ursula has just departed for. Lady Hyacinth is the grandest of the nobles in the Realm. And by grandest I mean the richest and the most powerful except for the King, and perhaps except for the Prince of Physics. Don't be fooled by Lady Ursula into thinking that all nobles here in Cogent Town are brainless fools." She smiled at Nikki's shocked expression. "Please excuse my harsh words. I am actually fond of Lady Ursula, in small doses. She can be sweet when she is in a good mood. But you must admit that she is brainless. Lady Hyacinth is another matter altogether. She has a powerful intellect and is a leader among the nobility. If she can be convinced of the danger you speak of then we may be able to prevent it. Lady Hyacinth will be able to raise the alarm. People will listen to her and believe her in a way that they would not listen to you or me."

Nikki nodded slowly. "Do you think she would agree to see us?"

"I think so," said the maid. "If my sister asks her to. My sister is her favorite servant. I think I can convince my sister to get you a few minutes alone with her Ladyship, but you must prepare your story well."

Nikki stared at the floor, lost in thought. The danger to Gwen and to the imps who lived in Cogent Town was probably not what she should emphasize. Lady Hyacinth would care more about her friends. Nobles who might lose their mansions. The problem was she didn't know which nobles were targets.

"Do you know which nobles might be sympathetic to the imps?" she asked Ava.

"Ah," said Ava. "So that is how it is. Rufius is a well-known imp-hater. So you believe that those nobles who have been friendly to the imps here in Cogent Town will be the targets of these fires."

Nikki nodded.

Ava went over to a dainty writing table in a corner of the parlor. An ink pot and a few pieces of parchment had been left on the tabletop. Ava dipped a quill in the ink pot and scribbled quickly on a piece of parchment. She handed it to Nikki. "It is not a complete list. It is only the names which occur to me off the top of my head. These are nobles who still invite imps to their dances and to their card games. Unfortunately the list is short and growing shorter every day, as Rufius has issued many decrees forbidding interaction with imps. Show this list to Lady Hyacinth and she will be able to act. If you can convince her of the danger, that is."

"I should go at once," said Nikki, standing up. "I don't know when the trouble might break out, but the person who informed me of it says it might be very soon. Even tonight."

Ava gave her a small, encouraging smile and beckoned Nikki to follow her. At the front door of the mansion she grabbed a black shawl from a coat rack and wrapped it around her.

"This page and I have a few errands to run for her Ladyship," Ava said to the footman guarding the front door the mansion. "I will be back before her Ladyship returns from the ball."

The mansion of the Duchess of Falsa had no outer wall surrounding it the way the mansion of the Prince of Physics did. And no armed guards either. Nikki realized that being a powerful figure in the Realm, as the Prince was, could have its downside. You had to watch your back all the time and constantly be concerned about your safety. It seemed like an exhausting way to live.

Ava led Nikki around the lilac bushes in the front garden and headed down the street. At first Nikki thought Ava was leading her toward the Fox and Fig, but they soon turned off into a maze of dark side-streets. Nikki tried to keep her bearings by watching the flickering lanterns far up on the high walls of Castle Cogent, but as the streets twisted and turned the castle seemed to change positions. She finally gave up and just blindly followed in Ava's footsteps.

After twenty minutes of walking Ava paused. They were in a

poor-looking area of the city where crumbling houses seemed to lean against each other for support. A hungry dog growled at them and Ava shooed it away with her apron.

"This is one of the areas where imps live," said Ava. "They used to live all over Cogent Town, but in these days of Maleficious and now Rufius they tend to live near each other for protection."

"Are we going to warn them to be on the watch for fires?" asked Nikki.

Ava shook her head. "No. Not right now. We can help them the most by informing Lady Hyacinth as soon as possible. I have only come this way because it is a shortcut to Clearwater Gardens, a lovely area of the city which borders the Clearwater River. It used to be part of the King's hunting grounds. Many of the grandest mansions of Cogent Town are located there. Lady Hyacinth's mansion is there, right on the banks of the river."

They were about to continue on when a sudden loud boom made them both jump. Windows all along the street rattled and a dog started barking.

"What was that?" asked Nikki, her heart pounding.

"I do not know," said Ava, looking wildly around. "The echoes are confusing. I cannot tell where the sound came from."

"There!" said Nikki, pointing above the rooftops surrounding them.

An orange glow lit up the sky.

"It is close by," said Ava. "This way." She darted down an alley lined with wooden carts and piles of firewood. Several alley cats dashed past them, headed in the opposite direction. As they approached the exit to the next street they could feel a wave of heat wash over them.

Nikki motioned Ava to stop and then cautiously poked her head around the side of the building at the end of the alley. The source of the heat was immediately obvious. Halfway down the narrow street a rickety wooden house several stories high was on fire. Part of its roof had already collapsed and the top story was exposed to the night sky. Imps in nightshirts and dressing gowns were frantically passing buckets of water from person to person along a chain of imps stretching from a town well to the burning building. Nikki pulled the collar of her page jacket over her nose, trying to block out the choking smoke. The smell of burning wood was mixed with something else, but it took Nikki a minute to recognize it. Sulfur. An ingredient of gunpowder.

Suddenly there was a whistling sound and another boom. The house next to the burning build caught fire. "Fireworks," said Nikki.

"What?" asked Ava, holding her apron over her nose and mouth.

"Fireworks," repeated Nikki. "They're kind of like torches that you can shoot into the air. That's how the fire was started. Come on. I saw where the second one came from." She started running down the street, ignoring Ava's questions. She had clearly seen a small blazing rocket launched from the roof of a building far down the street. She dodged through the chain of imps passing water buckets. A second chain had been started and someone yelled at her to help, but she knew that the best way to help was to prevent more fireworks from being launched.

Gasping from the smoke she skidded to a halt in front of a tall building built of rough granite. By the light of the fires she could just make out the sign over the door. Cogent Town Flour Mill. "Oh no!" she gasped.

"What is it?" asked Ava, catching up to her. "Go in! If this is the source of the fire torches we need to stop whoever is lighting them!"

"Flour!" Nikki exclaimed, pointing at the sign. "Flour dust

can explode!"

Ava pushed impatiently past her and yanked on the door of the flour mill. It opened with a groaning creak and the maid ran inside.

Nikki swore under her breath and followed her in. The words Gold Medal Flour echoed through her brain. Her high school history class had taken a field trip to Minneapolis to visit the Washburn Mill on the Mississippi River, the main mill of the Gold Medal Flour Company. In 1878 a spark had ignited flour dust floating in the air inside the mill. Eighteen people had been killed in the explosion and the mill had been completely destroyed. With someone shooting fireworks from the Cogent Town Flour Mill it was a miracle the building was still standing.

As her eyes adjusted to the darkness Nikki could see that the ground floor was empty. A huge, flat grinding stone in the center of the room was motionless. A wooden beam with a leather harness hanging from one end was attached to the center of the stone. A circle of hoof prints traced a pattern in the flour dust around the grinding stone. Nikki guessed that the mill used horses or donkeys to grind the flour. A surprising amount of flour dust was in the air, even though the mill was done grinding for the day. Nikki soon spotted the reason. A small window at the back of the room was open and a cold breeze was rushing in. It lifted the flour that coated everything and swirled it in the air. Nikki ran to the window and shut it tightly.

"Come on," whispered Ava, starting up the staircase to the second floor. "I can hear voices up above."

Nikki followed her, their footsteps sending up little clouds of flour dust.

They paused on the second floor landing. The only thing on that floor were hundreds of canvas bags full of flour. As they continued up the stairs to the third floor the voices up above became louder. Two men were arguing.

Nikki grabbed Ava's arm, pulling her to a stop. She recognized the voices. The harsh croak of an elderly man was Geber, the King's alchemist. And the hard, cruel voice raised in anger was the leader of the Mystic Men. Nikki shuddered as she remembered the vein pulsing in the empty socket of his missing eye.

"Launch another one!" shouted the Mystic man. "Let's take out the whole street and be done with it."

"No," croaked Geber. "We want this to be a warning to the imps. A strike of fear, not a full-on assault. Until Rufius is able to muster the Knights of the Iron Fist we don't have the man-power to stand up to both the King and the Prince of Physics. The King has been usefully idle but even he won't stand by if all of Cogent Town is burned to the ground. We need targeted fires, not a raging inferno."

"One or two more won't hurt," growled the Mystic leader.

There was a sound like flint scraping on stone and a brief flash of light illuminated the stairs where Nikki and Ava were standing.

"Wait!" croaked Geber. "You are too close to that open barrel! Get away from the dust!"

The blast shook the whole building. Nikki heard stones falling and glass shattering as she tumbled backwards down the stairs. She saw Ava fly past her through the air and then everything went black.

End of Book Seven

Nikki's adventures in the Realm of Reason come to a conclusion
in the eighth book of the *Logic to the Rescue* series.

The Logic to the Rescue series

Logic to the Rescue
The Prince of Physics
The Bard of Biology
Mystics and Medicine
The Sorcerer of the Stars
Warlock of the Wind
The Engineer of Evil

The Hamsters Rule series

Hamsters Rule, Gerbils Drool
Hamsters Rule the School

Excerpt from *Hamsters Rule, Gerbils Drool*

Chapter One

MELVIN STIRRED UNEASILY in his pile of sawdust shavings. The snuffly snores coming from the twin bed across the room were disturbing his rest. He crawled out of his nest and trundled down an orange plastic tunnel to a distant corner of his Hamster Habitat. Diving head first into a pile of cedar chips, he squirmed until only his chubby rear-end was visible. He twitched for a few seconds then settled back into sleep.

Melvin should have counted himself lucky. The snores of his owner, Miss Sally Jane Hesslop, who was eleven years old as of last Tuesday, were much quieter than usual due to Sally's head being buried under her *Xena Warrior Princess* bedspread. All that could be seen of Sally was a long strand of blonde hair with a wad of pink bubble gum stuck on the end of it.

The morning sun finished clearing the fog from San Francisco bay and lit up Sally's bedroom window. The light revealed quite a mess: Legos, comic books, sneakers, mismatched socks and a spilled can of Hungry Hamster Snacks were scattered across the floor. Sally was a firm believer in keeping all of her belongings in plain view. In an emergency (and most mornings were an emergency, as Sally had a talent for being late for school) precious time could be saved by getting dressed from the clothes on the floor.

This morning Sally's peaceful slumber was destined to last only a few more brief moments, for Robbie was out of bed and on the loose.

Robbie was Sally's four-year-old brother. He was famous up and down their neighborhood for his ability to eat anything dirt-related. Mud, clay, sand, litter box filler, anything lurking in the bottom of a flowerpot or fish tank, all were fair game. When it came to dirt Robbie was an omnivore. Though, of course, he had his favorites. The light fluffiness at the heart of the vacuum cleaner bag, the tasty compost at the roots of his grandmother's roses – these were special treats for special occasions, to be savored slowly and washed down with a good quality grape Kool Aid.

Today Robbie was up at his usual time of six a.m. He tiptoed into Sally's room, a stealthy menace in his footie pajamas and bike helmet. This helmet was a permanent item in Robbie's wardrobe. Robbie was fond of banging his head on things, so his father had started putting a helmet on him as soon as Robbie got out of bed.

Giggling softly and wielding a large rubber spatula, Robbie crept up to the snoring Sally. He pulled back the edge of the bedspread with one chubby fist and brought the spatula down with a satisfying thwhack on top of Sally's head.

"Aaaah!" Sally bolted upright, her scrawny arms swinging wildly as she tried to ward off her assailant. Her oversized *Xena* T-shirt billowed out, making her eighty-pound frame look twice its size. A yellow post-it note which was stuck to her forehead fluttered in the breeze as she whipped around and grabbed the spatula from a chortling Robbie. Sally rained down a barrage of blows with the spatula onto Robbie's bike helmet. Robbie made a dash for the door, knocking over a stack of comic books. He was almost to safety, inches from escape, when he miscalculated the distance between the door jamb and his head. He bounced backwards off the door, his helmet taking most of the punishment, tripped over a half-built castle made of Legos, and toppled over onto the carpet with his feet in the air.

Sally leapt out of bed with a wild war cry and rained rubbery blows down on Robbie as if beating a stubborn batch of dough.

"Sally Jane, are you out of bed yet?" The voice floating in from the hallway sounded in desperate need of coffee. Sally's father's dearest dream was to sleep in past six a.m., a dream which was destroyed on a daily basis by Robbie and his spatula. Robbie had assigned himself the task of family alarm clock and he took his job seriously. If the first whack on the head didn't wake his target at six on the dot then Robbie would tirelessly whack until he got results. Mr. Hesslop had tried hiding the spatula in the back of the cereal cupboard, but Robbie had just switched to whacking with the toilet brush. Mr. Hesslop had quickly decided that he preferred the spatula, the toilet brush tending to catch in his hair.

Sally gave Robbie one final blow then grabbed his pajama feet and dragged him out of her room. "I'm up, Dad. I'm up," she shouted, leaving Robbie lying on his back in the hallway. Sally darted back into her room and slammed the door. She yawned, scratched her ear with the captured spatula, and surveyed her wardrobe. Her favorite pair of jeans, only slightly muddy around the knees, hung off the end of her bed. She pulled them on and selected a pink T-shirt from a pile under the window. As she pulled it over her head the post-it which was stuck to her forehead fluttered to the floor. Sally scooped it up and read it aloud.

"Charlie Sanderson must pay. Skedyul revenge for recess."

Sally's blue eyes narrowed to slits, and she smacked her palm with the spatula.

"Right. It's payday, Charlie. Today, after third period."

"Okay, Robbie. You've had enough. Come and drink your juice."

Robbie, crouching over a scraggly fern which an aunt had given them for Christmas, ignored his Dad. He reached into the depths of the flowerpot and pulled up a fistful of loamy soil. He carefully picked off a ladybug which was crawling on his thumb and then crammed the dirt into his mouth.

Mr. Hesslop sighed. He grabbed Robbie off the floor and plopped him into a chair at the kitchen table. Mr. Hesslop was a taller version of Sally Jane. Both father and daughter had dishwater blond hair, blue eyes, long skinny arms and legs, and pointy elbows. Short, chubby Robbie, with his dark hair and brown eyes, looked completely unrelated to his Dad and his eleven-year-old sister, a fact which Sally mercilessly exploited. She had convinced Robbie that he was on loan from the bank that their Dad worked at, and that he could be returned at any time if she just said the word. Robbie had responded to this threat by reducing Sally's spatula wake-up calls to once a week. His Dad still got the seven-day-a-week treatment though. Robbie guessed correctly that his Dad loved him too much to pack him up and lock him in a bank vault.

"Robbie, you've got to stop eating dirt." Mr. Hesslop grabbed a paper napkin and wiped Robbie's muddy mouth. "Remember what Dr. Tompkins told you? If you don't stop you're going to have a tree growing in there." He tickled Robbie's stomach.

Robbie giggled. "Tree in tummy."

Sally wandered into the kitchen, bumping into the refrigerator. Her long, straight hair hung in front of her face like a curtain.

She had attempted to braid pieces of it, and the attempt had not gone well. One braid sprouted from the top of her head like an overgrown onion. Another looked like it was growing straight out of her ear. She sat down at the kitchen table, one hand tangled in the rest of her unbraided hair, the other grabbing for a box of Cheerios.

Mr. Hesslop passed her the milk. "Sally Jane, why don't you let me help you with your hair? I'll make you look real pretty."

What could be seen of Sally's face under her hair looked suspiciously like it was rolling its eyes. "Daaad. I'm not trying to look *pretty*. I'm doing Xena braids. See, if you're in a fight you don't want your hair in your face. You can't see good."

"What fight?" Mr. Hesslop said sharply, his thin nose pointed at his daughter like a fox on the scent.

Sally smiled innocently. "I was just being hypometical, Dad. Sheesh."

"Hypothetical," said Mr. Hesslop. "Robbie, don't do that." He grabbed Robbie's juice glass, which was now half empty. Robbie had poured the rest onto the floor and was straining against his father's arm, eager to get down from the table to study (and taste) the effects of orange juice on dirty linoleum at close range.

Melvin waddled into the kitchen, his fluffy orange fur dusting a path along the un-swept floor, his nose twitching for food. He disappeared under Sally's chair, dodged her swinging feet, and settled in front of the puddle of orange juice. His tiny pink tongue darted out and lapped at lightning speed, aware that even Mr. Hesslop with his lazy housekeeping skills was unlikely to leave a bonanza like this lying around for long.

Fortunately for Melvin, Mr. Hesslop was distracted by the sound of a knock at the front door. He set Robbie down and went to greet their visitor. A few seconds later he reappeared with Darlene Trockworthy, their next-door neighbor. A peroxide blond with heavy blue eye-shadow, a too-tight dress and too-high heels, Darlene occasionally babysat Robbie and Sally. Darlene and Robbie were best friends, mainly because Darlene let Robbie eat as much dirt as he wanted, but between Darlene and Sally it had been war from the start.

Darlene slid into a seat at the kitchen table, aiming a kick at Melvin on the way. "Is that rat loose again?" she asked, her mouth full of the toast she had grabbed off of Robbie's plate.

Sally glared at her. "He's not a rat, you dingbat."

"Sally, watch your manners," Mr. Hesslop said sharply.

"Bill, the kid's rhyming again. I thought you said she'd grow out of that." Darlene pouted at Mr. Hesslop, her bright red lipstick spattered with toast crumbs. The whole neighborhood knew that Darlene had her "sights set" on Bill Hesslop, but so far he had resisted her advances.

"She'll grow out of it eventually," said Mr. Hesslop. "It's just a phase. Robbie, don't do that."

Robbie had climbed off his chair and was sitting on the floor, rubbing Cheerios in the dust on the floor before eating them.

Mr. Hesslop picked him up. "I'll clean up Mr. Dirt Devil here and drop him at his preschool. Can you take Sally?"

The look Darlene shot Sally clearly said that she'd like to dump Sally in San Francisco bay. Darlene sighed heavily. "Yeah, sure." She pointed a warning finger at Sally, a long red fingernail raking the air like a claw. "But no rhyming, kid. I mean it. One Iambic what-ya-ma-callit and I'm selling you to the slave traders. They'll ship you to Nebraska and make you shuck corn 'til you're eighty."

Sally smiled at her sweetly. "Your wish is my command. And your head is filled with sand." Sally scooped Melvin up, put him on her shoulder, and marched out of the kitchen.

"Put that rat back in his cage." Darlene yelled after her. "And if you're not ready in ten minutes I'm leaving without you."

Chapter Two

SALLY AND DARLENE maintained a careful no-touching distance as they headed down the hill to Sally's school. When a bike rider on the sidewalk forced them to shrink the gap between them they automatically sprang apart again after the bike had passed, as if repelled by a magnetic field.

Darlene examined her makeup in a compact mirror as she teetered along, causing oncoming pedestrians to grumble as they jumped out of her way. Sally practiced karate kicks, viciously attacking the most dangerous looking trash cans and mailboxes along their route, her backpack flopping wildly on her shoulders.

Halfway down the hill a posse of poodles suddenly rushed out the front door of a tall apartment building and made straight for Sally. Sally threw herself down on her knees and scooped up the scruffy little white poodle which was leading the pack. The little poodle yapped excitedly, licking Sally's face. The other three poodles were tall, black, and dignified, with the fur on their heads shaped into elegant topknots. They sniffed at Sally's backpack and at Darlene's shoes. One of them lifted his leg and took aim at Darlene's stiletto. Darlene shrieked and jumped back.

"Brutus! No!"

A chubby little girl about Sally's age ran up to them and grabbed the peeing poodle. She had black curly hair and large dark eyes. She was wearing a plaid skirt, a starched white blouse, and black patent leather shoes which looked extremely uncomfortable. "Brutus, you bad dog! Sorry, Miss Trockworthy. My Mom's trying to train him not to pee on everyone, but he forgets sometimes." She herded the poodles back up the front steps of the apartment building. "C'mon Brutus, Caesar, Nero, and Fluffy. You can't come to school with us. Poodles are not allowed. Go back upstairs."

Sally waved goodbye to Fluffy and stood up, dusting off her knees. "Hi, Katie! Are you ready to rumble?"

The chubby girl looked at her in confusion. "Huh?"

Sally skipped around Katie, chanting. "Charlie's a boy, so he's not too bright. We'll shout with joy when we win this fight."

Katie picked up the book bag she had dropped during the poodle roundup. A worried frown crinkled her pale forehead. "I don't know, Sally. Remember what happened the last time you got into a fight at school? Billy Lauder's tooth got knocked out and Arnold the Iguana ate it and had to go to the Pet Hospital. I don't want Arnold to go to the Pet Hospital. He doesn't like it there. Remember the time I put my Mom's Lilac Mist hand lotion on him because he looked dry? I thought it would make him feel better, but it turned him all pink and he had to go to the Pet Hospital so they could make him green again. Arnold hates being pink. Pink is a girl's color, and Arnold's a boy iguana. Mr. Zukas says so. So you shouldn't fight."

Katie looked ready to cry. Her large eyes grew red-rimmed and shiny. Sally patted her on the shoulder and handed her a wadded up Kleenex which she pulled out of her backpack. She resumed skipping in circles.

"Arnold's not going to the Pet Hospital this time," said Sally. "I have a new Secret Revenge Plan, and there aren't any iguanas in the plan."

Katie sniffed and wiped her nose. She followed Sally and

Darlene as they continued down the hill. "Oh. Well, I guess it's okay then. I'm glad Arnold isn't in your new Secret Revenge Plan, cause iguanas don't like fighting."

They reached the bottom of the hill and turned onto a narrow side street lined with gingko trees. The sidewalk was covered with fan-shaped gingko leaves. Sally swooshed at them with the toes of her sneakers, sending the leaves swirling like tiny doves. Katie carefully stepped on the bare patches of sidewalk, keeping her shiny patent leather shoes free of leaf mush. Up ahead the street was jammed with cars disgorging kids with backpacks. The kids ran into the fenced-in playground of Montgomery Elementary School, a three-story brick building with sturdy granite columns flanking its front door. The building had a basketball court on one side and a cluster of crooked pine trees on the other side.

"Okay, you two," said Darlene, finally closing her compact. "Get lost. One of your parents will pick you up after school. Don't know which parent. Don't care." She sauntered off, popping a wad of gum into her mouth. Sally stuck her tongue out at Darlene's retreating back.

"You shouldn't do that," said Katie, gasping in horror. "My Mom says that kids should always show adults the proper respect."

Sally snorted. "Darlene's not an adult. She's a doofus." She skipped around Katie, chanting. "Darlene, Darlene, she's not too keen. She's the biggest dunce you've ever seen."

Katie turned red. She quickly looked around to make sure that Darlene hadn't heard. Darlene was examining her nails as she walked away, completely oblivious to the kids dodging around her on the sidewalk. Katie breathed a sigh of relief and followed Sally into the school building.

"Okay, everyone settle down!" Mr. Zukas' deep voice boomed over the chaos in his fifth-grade classroom. He gave his sweater vest a firm tug and strode to the front of the class. "Get to your desks, pronto. Tommy, get your foot out of Kyle's mouth. Patricia, give Tiffany back her shoes. They're too small for you anyway, you clodhopper."

Thirty kids rushed to their seats with a sound like elephants tap dancing. Sally threw herself into her assigned seat in the front row of desks. Katie lowered herself demurely into the seat directly behind Sally. Arnold the Iguana calmly surveyed the classroom from his cage at the back.

Mr. Zukas opened a fat textbook. As he slowly searched for the page he wanted Sally started to fidget. She squirmed like an eel, sat on her hands, and finally couldn't contain herself any longer. She raised her arm and began waving it furiously back and forth. Mr. Zukas ignored her and turned another page.

Never one to be discouraged, Sally climbed onto her chair and waved both arms wildly like a pint-sized airport worker guiding a jumbo jet into a parking space.

"Sally Jane Hesslop," sighed Mr. Zukas, not looking up, "get down off of there before you break your neck. Not that I would mind, but the principal gets grumpy when students kick the bucket."

"Sorry, Mr. Zukas," said Sally, climbing down. "I just had a question. Can we have more discusses on evolution? Cause I looked it up on Google and a Google person says we came from tadpoles. I think it would be cool to be a tadpole. I had a tadpole once. I kept it in a Sprite bottle. After I drank the Sprite, of course. But then my brother Robbie drank the tadpole. Are we having fish sticks for lunch today?"

Mr. Zukas rubbed his forehead, looked longingly at the clock, and sighed again. "I haven't checked the lunch menu today, Sally. It's posted on the cafeteria door. You can check at recess. And no, we don't come from tadpoles. We are primates, which means we are related to the great apes. Our closest cousins are the chimpanzees. All of which I told you yesterday, and which you'd remember if you'd been paying attention. Now, class, open your history books to page thirty-four. The Pioneers. They crossed the Great Plains in covered wagons. Conditions were harsh. They had to hunt for their food."

A small red-haired boy wearing a shirt and tie waved politely from the desk next to Sally.

"Yes, Rodney?" asked Mr. Zukas. "Did you have a question?"

"Not a question, Mr. Zukas. Just a remark. It might interest the class to know that the Pioneers frequently ate deer as well as buffalo. They shot them with rifles."

Mr. Zukas beamed at him. "That's right, Rodney. I'm glad someone's been doing their homework."

Rodney smirked proudly while behind him the rest of the class rolled their eyes.

"Can anyone else tell me what other animals the Pioneers might have hunted?" asked Mr. Zukas.

Sally waved furiously.

"Anyone at all?" Mr. Zukas asked somewhat desperately.

Sally bounced up and down in her seat, arm still waving.

Mr. Zukas sighed. "Yes, Sally."

"They ate gophers."

Loud expressions of disgust erupted from the rest of the class. Sally turned around and glared at them.

"I'm fairly certain the Pioneers didn't eat gophers, Sally," said Mr. Zukas. "I believe gophers are inedible."

"Nuh-*uh*," said Sally. "Gophers are super edible. The Pioneers roasted them over campfires and put hot sauce on them. They tasted like corn dogs. Only furry."

"Eeeww." The rest of the class unanimously decided it was grossed out. Rodney cleared his throat and looked disdainfully at Sally.

"In the unlikely event that the Pioneers ate gophers," said Rodney with a sneer, "they would have skinned them first. The fur would have been removed before roasting."

"Nuh-uh," retorted Sally. "The fur's where all the vitamins are. Just like potatoes. You keep the skin on for the vitamins."

Behind Sally, Katie gasped and put her hand over her mouth. She had turned a sickly shade of green.

Mr. Zukas peered at her. "Katie, do you need to use the Little Girl's Room?"

Katie nodded tearfully at him. He waved impatiently in the direction of the door and Katie dashed out of the classroom.

Mr. Zukas sighed and turned a page in his textbook. "Let's get off the topic of the Pioneers' diet. Class, have a look at the picture on the next page. See the tin star this man is wearing? That meant he was a sheriff. He kept order in the lawless Wild West. Of course, it was a difficult job, and he needed lots of help. Frequently he would deputize. That means to create a kind of temporary sheriff. Who do you think he deputized?"

"Hamsters," said Sally at once.

Mr. Zukas pulled at his tie, looking like he was tempted to strangle himself with it. "Hamsters cannot be deputies or anything else in the law enforcement arena, Sally. Hamsters are furry rodents, just like gophers."

Sally's eyes flashed dangerously. "Hamsters are nothing like gophers! Hamsters and gophers are sworn enemies. Just ask my hamster, Melvin. You don't want to get him started on gophers.

He gets so mad his fur stands straight up and he hops around like microwave popcorn. Besides, hamsters can *so* be in the law enforcement arena. Melvin is in the law enforcement arena. He's a Secret Agent. He has a Secret Agent JetPack and everything. He straps it on and flies around San Francisco looking for bad guys. If he finds any bad guys he zaps them with his Secret Agent Laser Gun." Sally jumped up and aimed an imaginary laser gun at Mr. Zukas. "Kerpow!"

Mr. Zukas sighed and put a hand on his forehead. "Recess is early today," he said. "Everyone clear out of here. And stay out until the bell rings. I don't care if a tornado sweeps through the schoolyard. If anyone so much as puts one toe inside this classroom in the next half hour I'll personally feed them to the monster that lives in the school basement. He loves to snack on little kids. Especially ones who own hamsters."

"THERE HE IS. Charlie Sanderson, Snot Extraordinaire. Are you ready?" Sally was on the Jungle Gym, hanging upside down by her knees. One of her braids had come undone and her long hair was covering her face. She parted it with her hands and peered at a blond-haired boy walking past. He was wearing baggy pants, expensive sneakers, and a backwards baseball cap and was surrounded by a bunch of boys dressed exactly like him.

Katie peered up at Sally worriedly from a safe perch on the lowest bar of the Jungle Gym. She had her skirt neatly tucked under her legs and her shiny patent leather shoes were carefully resting on a clean patch of grass. "Ready for what?" she asked.

"The Plan," whispered Sally.

"You never told me the plan. I don't know what to do. You just said you had a Secret Revenge Plan, and that there were no Iguanas."

"That's right," said Sally. "We don't need an Iguana for this plan, which is a good thing because Arnold the Iguana is retiring from the revenge business. Arnold had a little chat with Melvin at one of their Secret Agent meetings in the school cafeteria. Arnold told Melvin that he was getting too old for Secret Revenge Plans. He's going to retire to a home for elderly Iguanas in Florida. They spend all day sleeping in hammocks and drinking chocolate milkshakes. Melvin tried to talk him out of it. Mel's afraid Arnold will get fat from all the chocolate milkshakes, but Arnold's already pretty fat because Emily Niederbacher keeps feeding him her peanut butter and jelly sandwiches." Sally grabbed the Jungle Gym bar with both hands, flipped her legs through and dropped to the ground. "We don't need Arnold for this particular Secret Revenge Plan. You can be my back up. Follow me."

Katie sighed and reluctantly followed Sally across the playground.

Sally swerved around a group of kids playing hopscotch and sauntered in the direction of Charlie Sanderson and his posse, who were leaning against the schoolyard's chain-link fence and attempting to look cool. One of the boys nudged Charlie in the ribs and pointed at Sally.

Sally walked up to Charlie and slapped him on the back. "How's it going, Sanderson?"

The posse laughed and Charlie angrily pushed Sally away. "Get away from me, Hesslop, you freak."

Sally smiled. "I may be a freak, but you're a geek. And may I say, you really reek."

Charlie tried to shove her again, but Sally dodged away. She waved at Charlie as he and his posse stalked off to a far corner of the playground. Sally pulled something out of her pocket and tied it to the chain-link fence.

"What are you doing?" whispered Katie. "Are we going to get in trouble again? I can't go to the Principal's office again. I just can't. Mrs. Finsterman always says she's going to pinch my arm with that clothes pin she keeps on her desk."

"She won't pinch you," said Sally, watching the boys depart.

"How do you know? She always says she will."

"I know 'cause she always says she's going to pinch me too, but she never does. It's a psychotogical strategy, like when Xena pretended to be a goddess and the Mud People worshipped her."

Katie stared at her in bafflement. "Mrs. Finsterman is a Mud Person?"

Sally put a finger to her mouth to shush Katie and pointed at the group of boys. Charlie and his gang were about twenty yards away, torturing a first-grader by throwing pebbles at him. The first-grader hopped around like a frightened puppy, not sure whether to cry or run.

Sally checked the fence and muttered to herself. "Two more feet. Come on, you poophead. Keep walking."

Katie frowned at her in confusion. She peered at the group of boys then bent down to examine the fence. "Sally, what . . ."

Sally waved her arms to shush her. The school bell rang, signaling the end of recess. Kids started running for the doors. Charlie Sanderson and his posse followed at a leisurely pace. Suddenly Charlie halted, frowning. He pulled at the waistline of his baggy pants, shrugged, and took another step. Sally yanked Katie away from the fence, giggling wildly. She ran into the school building, pulling Katie along behind her.

A huge burst of laughter suddenly erupted from the school yard. Sally stood on her tiptoes and peeked out of the glass window in the front door of the building. Charlie Sanderson was standing in the middle of the playground with his baggy pants down around his ankles and his *Finding Nemo* underpants on display for all to see. Kids pointed at him, wetting themselves from laughing. Grinning wickedly, Sally pulled a small piece of fishing line from her pocket and showed it to Katie.

Chapter Three

S ALLY WAS LYING on the floor of the Hesslop's living room, peering under an armchair. Muttering under her breath, she reached under the chair and pulled out a slinky and a blackened banana peel. Behind her, Robbie was sitting in the middle of the room wearing Snoopy underpants and his bike helmet. He giggled and whacked himself on the head with a toilet brush, matching the rhythm of Michael Jackson's *Beat it*, which was playing on the radio.

Sally sighed. The armchair was not delivering the goods. She crawled over to the sofa. Darlene Trockworthy was sitting there with her legs stretched out on the coffee table, painting her toenails. As she crawled under Darlene's legs Sally accidentally bumped them. A streak of Cotton Candy pink shot across Darlene's toes and up her ankle.

"Damn it, kid," groused Darlene, "Watch what you're doing. You made me mess up my pedicure."

"Sorry," Sally mumbled grudgingly. "It's just that I can't find Melvin. Have you seen him?"

"Nope, and good riddance," said Darlene. "That rodent's always creeping around underfoot. I swear he tries to trip me on purpose."

Sally sat back on her heels and smirked at Darlene. "He does that 'cause it's part of his Secret Mission. He's Special Agent

Melvin, and he goes to Washington BC every weekend for Super Secret Hamster Orders. He's trained to trip all enemy combatants."

Darlene wiped the nail polish off her foot. "Well, if you can't find him maybe he's at the White House meeting the President," she said. "I hear they serve hamster every Friday."

Sally gave her an evil glare and flopped on her stomach to peer under the sofa.

Behind her Melvin suddenly appeared, rolling across the living room on an old-fashioned four-wheeled roller skate. His chubby rear-end didn't quite fit on the skate, and he dusted a path across the floor with his fur. He rolled from one end of the room to the other and disappeared into the kitchen. Robbie waved the toilet brush at him as he passed.

Sally pulled her head out from under the sofa and hopped to her feet. She planted her fists on her hips. "Drat you, Melvin. Where *are* you? If you're hiding in the microwave again I'm going to spank your little furry butt. You know Dad hates it when his microwave popcorn tastes like hamster."

She stomped into the kitchen and opened the microwave. No Melvin. She banged open cupboards and rattled pans. "Melvin, if you've gone on a Secret Mission again you are soooo in trouble. You know you aren't supposed to go on Secret Missions after your bedtime. I'm gonna write to Washington. They'll remote you back to Janitor Melvin and take away your Secret Agent Jetpack."

Sally crawled under the kitchen table and peered inside an empty box of Wheaties. Behind her Melvin had managed (by methods known only to himself and other Secret Agent Hamsters) to get himself on top of the fridge. He poked his nose over the side and surveyed the perilous drop to the kitchen counter. After a moment's hesitation, he stepped off the fridge, executing a perfect swan dive with a half-twist. He landed face-first on the kitchen counter then slowly toppled over onto his back, legs in the air. He tried to roll onto his feet but was hampered by a touch of middle-aged spread. After several tries he got himself right-side up and waddled to the edge of the countertop. At that moment Robbie wandered in, fencing with his toilet brush. Melvin took a step into the unknown and landed splat on top of Robbie's bike helmet, all four feet splayed out and hanging on for dear life. Oblivious to his stowaway, Robbie fenced back into the living room, taking Melvin with him.

"Sally, get off the floor," said Mr. Hesslop as he entered the kitchen, a pencil behind his ear and the grumpy look of a man who's just been wrestling with his tax returns. "You're as bad as Robbie. Remember, you're supposed to set a good example for him. Now, go brush your teeth. It's bedtime."

Sally scrambled out from under the table and saluted. "Sir. Yes Sir. Your orders we obey. We're here to save the day. Good dental hygiene is a must. We'll clean our teeth or bust." She marched out of the kitchen, humming a martial tune. At the end of the hall she pivoted sharply and entered a small bathroom whose plumbing fixtures dated from the fifties. A bulging hamper full of wet towels sat in the corner and a flotilla of rubber ducks was lined up along the edge of the bathtub. The back of the toilet overflowed with half-empty shampoo bottles.

Sally knelt and began throwing towels out of the hamper. "Melvin, you varmint, you're about to become a garment. My Xena doll needs a fur coat, and you've got my vote."

She stuck her head into the now empty hamper. Behind her Melvin sauntered into the bathroom and scrambled up onto the edge of the tub, climbing the pyramid of wet towels Sally had dumped on the floor. He wound his way along the rim of the bathtub, which was full of soapy water leftover from Robbie's bath. Melvin dodged the rubber ducks with surprising agility, but overconfidence got the better of him and he slipped, falling into the bathtub with a splash.

Sally pulled her head out of the hamper and rushed over. "Melvin, you poophead. Your Secret Agent Swimming Lessons aren't til next week."

A stream of bubbles floating up from under the water was the only answer. Sally scooped Melvin up and deposited him on the bathroom rug. Melvin shook like a tiny dog and sat shivering, his orange fur matted to his sides.

"It's okay, Mel," said Sally. "I'll fix you right up with my Top Secret Air Blaster."

She grabbed a blow drier and turned it on High. The blast of hot air rolled Melvin over backward. He did a full somersault and ended up on standing on his head against the side of the bathtub. Sally picked him up and aimed the blow drier at his tummy. His fur blew straight backward as if he was in a hurricane. When Sally had finished drying him he was twice his normal size and had the hamster version of an Afro.

"Melvin! That's a great disguise. You can use it on your next undercover mission. Nobody will ever recognize you. You can be Horace the Hairdresser, famous for your skills with a curling iron. All the lady hamsters will be lining up to make an appointment with you."

Melvin's Afro started to deflate.

"Hang on Melvin," said Sally. "You just need some Product to maintain volume. That's what those hair commercials on TV are always saying."

Sally grabbed a can of hair mousse from the cabinet under the sink and sprayed a big glob on Melvin, who promptly disappeared under a pile of foam. Sally dug him out of the foam and rubbed the mousse into his fur, then snatched a toothbrush from the sink. "This is Dad's. He won't mind," said Sally as she brushed Melvin's fur into spikes. She sat him back down on the bathroom rug.

"There! You totally look like a cool dude. You look like one of those singers on American Idol. You just need to learn how to dance."

Sally jumped up and launched into a wild dance step. Melvin backed into a corner as Sally's flailing arms whacked the shower curtain and knocked a shampoo bottle into the toilet. Sally finished with a flourish and bowed low before an imaginary audience. "C'mon Mel. It's not hard. You just do little wiggle and a little rap. You just gotta have attitude. Like this."

Sally grabbed a rubber duck and sang into it like a microphone. "My name's Sally J. and I'm here to say, I'm doing my dance 'cause I pulled down Charlie's pants."

Sally picked up Melvin and danced around with him. "You need a hamster rap. All the tough hamsters have one. And maybe some bling. I wonder if Dad would buy you a gold chain."

Melvin looked decidedly skeptical about this, not to mention seasick from all the dancing.

Sally danced into her bedroom, singing. "I'm furry and I'm cute. I'm a Secret Agent to boot. I've got a special JetPack which is totally wack."

She tucked Melvin into his Hamster Habitat. Melvin trundled down the orange tube to his usual nest, his sticky moussed fur attracting bits of sawdust. By the time he reached his nest in the middle of the Habitat he looked like a tiny pile of kindling.

"Another super disguise, Mel," said Sally. "Totally cool. You can do your next Secret Mission at Tony's Pizza. They have sawdust all over their floor. They'll never spot you. You can sneak into the kitchen and find out the ingredients of their Secret Pizza Sauce."

Melvin burrowed into the sawdust of his nest until he was just a sawdust-lump. Sally yawned and blew him a kiss. "Night Mel."

Chapter Four

"**S**ALLY JANE HESSLOP, you are a demon spawn."

Mrs. Patterson, leader of Brownie Troop 112, wiped the milk off her sour face and glared down at Sally. The two of them were faced off in the middle of the Montgomery Elementary School cafeteria. A table with cartons of milk and a plate of Rice Krispie Treats was setup in one corner.

The wayward milk had ended up on Mrs. Patterson's face through totally unavoidable circumstances. Sally had been chasing another Brownie while holding a carton of milk and a straw. Squirting had been inevitable.

Sally planted her fists on her hips and regaled Mrs. Patterson with a cold stare. They were old enemies. They had disliked each other from the very first day that Mrs. Patterson had assumed the leadership of the troop. On that fateful day Sally had been showing the other brownies how to slide along the newly polished wooden floor in their stocking feet. She had just launched into a particularly energetic slide when Mrs. Patterson had walked through the door of the cafeteria. The resulting collision had knocked Mrs. Patterson off her feet and onto her support-hose covered knees. Mrs. Patterson had been trying to transfer Sally to another Brownie troop ever since, so far without success.

"Well," said Sally, "if I'm a demon spawn then I bet it's a cool demon, one that can shoot flames out of its eyeballs. I wish I could shoot flames out of my eyeballs. I'd turn Charlie Sanderson into a crispy critter."

Mrs. Patterson raised her eyes to the heavens. "When I say that you are a demon spawn, Sally Jane Hesslop, it means that you are a very bad girl. One of the worst I've had the misfortune to meet in all my years of guiding Brownies along the difficult path to becoming young ladies."

Sally fiddled with her straw. "I'd rather be a demon spawn than a young lady. I bet demon spawn have cool super powers. The coolest super power would be to turn people into potato bugs. My first victim would be Charlie Sanderson. If I turned him into a potato bug it would be a big improvement. I'd probably get a medal from the President. Then they'd have a parade for me and I'd ride on a float past the White House and wave to the crowd. Like this." Sally energetically waved her arms, spraying drops of milk onto Mrs. Patterson's bouffant hairdo.

Mrs. Patterson closed her eyes and kneaded her forehead with two shaking fingers. "Sally Jane Hesslop, we were discussing you spewing milk everywhere and making a mess, not super powers and potato bugs. Now go get some paper towels from the restroom and wipe this up."

"Okay" said Sally, shrugging. She tucked the straw under her Brownie beanie. "When do we get to make bird feeders from pinecones? That's in the Brownie handbook, you know. Page forty-nine. You stick peanut butter in the pinecones so the birds can peck it out. Though I don't understand why we can't just spread the peanut butter on Ritz crackers. Then the birds could peck it real easy. Molly Sanderson says it's because the birds like to work hard for their food, but that's just stupid. Besides, Molly is Charlie Sanderson's sister and she picks her nose, so you know anything she says is suspected. That's what my Dad says. Nose pickers are Dim Bulbs and to be suspected. The crackers don't have to be Ritz. Wheat Thins would work good too."

Mrs. Patterson sighed. "Sally Jane Hesslop, I don't know what you're blathering on about. Get this mess cleaned up. *Now*."

Mindy Nichols, a thin black girl with red bows on the ends of her cornrows, ran up to Sally. She peered after the departing Mrs. Patterson with a fearful expression. "Sally, guess what? Mrs. Osterman isn't coming today. She's in the hospital."

Mrs. Osterman was the co-leader of the troop. She was a quiet young woman with a warm smile who was liked by all the Brownies.

"You mean it's just us and Prissy Patterson?" groaned Sally. "Oh barf. Why is Mrs. Osterman in the hospital?"

"Molly Sanderson says it's because she's having an *operation*," whispered Mindy.

Sally rolled her eyes. "Molly is always saying stupid stuff. You know that. She's a Sanderson. You can't believe anything she says. C'mon. Let's go ask Sandra Chang. She'll know."

Sally and Mindy ran up to a group of girls gathered around Sandra Chang, a tall, graceful Chinese girl with a curtain of shiny black hair hanging all the way to her hips. A purple silk scarf was artfully tied around the neck of her Brownie uniform.

Sally barged her way through the group. "Hey Sandra."

Sandra nodded at her graciously, like a benevolent Queen acknowledging her subjects.

"Sandra, what's up with Mrs. Osterman? Mindy says she's in the hospital."

"I'm sorry, Sally," replied Sandra Chang in a quiet, authoritative voice. "I don't know the details. All I know is that Mrs. Patterson is taking over as Troop Leader."

Loud groans erupted from all the Brownies within earshot. Molly Sanderson, a short, pudgy blond girl with two front teeth missing, sister to the infamous Charlie Sanderson, jumped up and down frantically, waving her hand as if in school.

"Thandra. Thandra," lisped Molly, "I know what'th happened to Mrs. Othterman. My brother Charlie told me."

On hearing Charlie's name Sally made loud gagging noises and clutched her throat. Molly ignored her, looking intently at Sandra. Finally Sandra gave her a regal nod.

"Mrs. Othterman ith having a Hystertology," whispered Molly excitedly. "That'th an operation. It meanth thee can't have babiesth anymore, unlesth she goeth to Mexico and getsth it reverthed. Then her babiesth will come out backwardsth, like when your Dad backth the car out of the garage. Latht week my Dad backed our car out of the garage and ran over my brother'th bicycle. My Dad said a very bad wordth."

Sally planted her hands on her hips and gave Molly a look of scathing contempt. "That's not a Hystertology, Sanderson. A Hystertology is when you have your ears pinned back. The doctor staples them to your head so you don't look like Dumbo."

"Mrs. Othterman doesthn't look like Dumbo," said Molly.

"Well, not anymore," shot back Sally. "She's had a Hystertology. Sheesh, Sanderson. You are such a dimwit sometimes. I guess it runs in the family."

Molly advanced on her, fists clenched. "You take that back Hessthlop."

Sally assumed a Xena fighting pose. "C'mon, Sanderson. I'll lick you, and then I'll go lick your stupid brother."

"Charlie's a twit,
He's Molly's brother.
He has half a wit,
Molly has the other."

Sally raised her leg in preparation for a super-duper martial arts kick. Molly stood her ground for a second, then thought better of it and dashed off to find Mrs. Patterson.

"Girls! Girls!" shouted Mrs. Patterson from the center of the cafeteria. "Everyone gather round. It's Share Time. Bring the item you're going to share with the group over here."

There was a noisy scramble as all the Brownies rushed to a pile of backpacks stacked against the wall, and then convened in the center of the room. They threw themselves on the wooden floor in a cross-legged circle around Mrs. Patterson.

"Molly, dear, why don't you go first," said Mrs. Patterson.

Molly Sanderson smirked at the others and walked to the center of the circle. She held up a Barbie doll dressed in an immaculate princess-type costume of white silk with a red velvet cape. "Thith ith Princeth Thophie of Bavaria. Thee's dressthed for the ball. Thee's a Spethial Edition. My Mom bought her for me in New York at Bloomingdaleth."

"She's just beautiful, Molly," said Mrs. Patterson. "So precious. I bet all the young ladies here want to be Princesses, don't you, girls?"

Sally sprang up. "Of course. I'm Princess Scary Fighting Eagle from the Moping Moose tribe. We get dressed for balls too. We paint our faces with red stripes, stick eagle feathers in our ears, and do our Special Moose Waltz around the campfire."

Sally launched into a fast-paced dance, shaking her arms and kicking her legs over her head. Her Brownie beanie flew off, and girls scrambled backwards as she lunged wildly toward them. She concluded by spinning rapidly in a circle, then staggered dizzily back to her spot on the floor.

Mrs. Patterson closed her eyes during this performance. After Sally had sat down again she opened her eyes, a pained expression on her face. "Mindy," she sighed, "why don't you go next?"

Mindy Nichols moved to the center of the circle, bashfully

pulling at her cornrows. She pulled a brightly colored paper bird from a bag. Several of the Brownies oohed and aahed. Mindy smiled gratefully. "This is a Japanese art called Origami. My Mom learned it when she was stationed at a Navy base in Sasebo, Japan. She taught it to me. This is a tsuru. That's Japanese for crane. All the kids in Japan learn to make them. The crane is a symbol of peace." Mindy sat down abruptly, looking embarrassed. The Brownies applauded.

Mrs. Patterson pursed her lips as if she'd just drunk lemon juice. "Very, er, multi-cultural, Mindy. Though maybe you should bring something a little more American next time. These exotic things aren't really Brownie appropriate for Brownie meetings. Let's see, Sandra, why don't you come up."

Sandra Chang nodded and rose gracefully to her feet. She unrolled a paper scroll which displayed a vertical line of beautiful Chinese characters. "This is called calligraphy. It's a very popular art in China. These characters are in the Mandarin language, which my mother and grandmother speak. My grandmother taught me how to do calligraphy. We use a pot of black ink and a brush made of sheep's hair."

Sandra sat down and the Brownies applauded respectfully.

"My goodness," said Mrs. Patterson, "This is certainly an international group. I feel like I'm at the United Nations. Well, onward. Who'd like to volunteer?"

Sally waved her arm wildly. Another Brownie across from Sally dared to raise her arm as well. Sally glared daggers at her opponent, and the offending Brownie promptly dropped her challenge and looked like she'd be thrilled to sink into the floor. Mrs. Patterson tried mightily to avoid Sally's gaze, but resistance was futile. Sally marched unbidden to the center of the circle, carrying a paper takeout carton. Mrs. Patterson raised her eyes heavenward.

"I'll go next, Mrs. Patterson," said Sally. She opened the carton and pulled out something wriggly. The Brownies gasped in horror and the ones closest scooted away. Molly Sanderson screamed.

"Mrsth. Pattersthon, Thally'th brought a rat! Eeeuww. Make her take ith away!"

Sally rolled her eyes. "It's not a rat, Sanderson, you doofus. It's my hamster, Melvin. My Dad shaved him. See, what happened was, I put some of Darlene Trockworthy's Super Hold Hair Mousse on him. Darlene wants to be my Dad's girlfriend, and she left her hair mousse in our bathroom."

Mrs. Patterson clutched the pearls around her neck and muttered something about tramps.

"Anyway," continued Sally, "it turns out you should never mousse a hamster. It glues their fur up something awful. Plus you should especially never put mousse on your hamster and then let him roll around in sawdust. My Dad said there must have been some kind of chemical reaction between the pine sap in the sawdust and Darlene's Super Hold Hair Mousse. It hardened up like that shellac stuff we used on our birdhouses last year. Poor Mel here couldn't even walk. He just rolled around like a pinecone with feet. So my Dad used his electric razor and shaved off all of Melvin's fur. So now Mel's got a crew cut, like an Army guy. Anybody want to hold him?"

The Brownies all recoiled. Melvin dove back into the takeout container as Mrs. Patterson stepped forward and made shooing motions at Sally. Sally reluctantly relinquished center stage and sat back down. She dropped a Rice Krispie Treat into the takeout carton. "It's okay, Mel," she whispered into the carton, "Don't mind Prissy Patterson. The troop loved you. You were a big hit."

Chapter Five

———◆———

"I WISH YOU could have been there, Katie. Melvin was the star of the show. It was like American Idol, but with hamsters."

Sally and Katie were walking across a wide green lawn. Sally was wearing baggy blue shorts and a T-shirt that said "Girl Power!" in sparkly red and blue letters. On her feet she had one red basketball sneaker and one black one. Katie was uncomfortably over-dressed, as usual, in a starched white blouse with a Peter Pan collar, a kilt, and black patent-leather Mary Janes. Sally was swinging a takeout container by its wire handle.

"American what?" asked Katie.

"Oh jeez Katie. Are your parents *ever* going to let you watch TV?"

"Probably not. They say it turns your brain into Swiss Cheese."

"That's just stupid," said Sally. "Everyone knows that brains are made out of spaghetti. Don't you remember Mindy's Halloween party? We had to put our hands in the brains, and they were spaghetti. Cooked spaghetti, of course. Nobody has raw spaghetti for brains, except maybe Charlie Sanderson. Hey, want to see Melvin's outfit?"

She stopped and set the takeout container down on the grass. When she opened it Melvin popped his head out, his whiskers twitching. He was wearing a purple and white striped doggie sweater. Sally picked him up and held him out to Katie, who scratched his shaved head. Melvin yawned and had a good stretch, waving his tiny tail back and forth, which was the only part of him which still had fur on it. Sally put him on her shoulder. "Isn't this sweater cute? Mel was cold without his fur, so my Dad bought it at a pet store. They didn't have any hamster sweaters, so he got this one. It's for Chihuahua puppies. Melvin didn't want to wear kid's clothes, but I finally talked him into it."

"It's very stylish," said Katie.

"You bet," said Sally, scratching Melvin's nose. "Mel's a stylin' dude. I wish you could have been at our Brownie meeting. We had Show and Tell. Sandra Chang brought some fancy writing called colonoscopy, cause she's Chinese. Mindy Nichols brought this paper bird called a guru. You could have brought that droodle toy. I don't get why your parents hate the Brownies."

"It's a dreidel, not a droodle. And my parents don't hate the Brownies. They just don't like Mrs. Patterson. They don't like the way she's always telling people they aren't American."

"Yeah, she's stuck on that," said Sally. "My Dad says she's got a psychotological problem about it. A Pixation. That's when Pixies get inside your head and turn your brain into scrambled eggs. Hey, if Mrs. Patterson watches a lot of TV and your parents are right about the Swiss Cheese, then her brain will turn into a cheese omelet."

They passed through a garden full of pink and yellow roses. In front of them loomed an imposing mansion flanked by towering oak trees. A driveway bordered with rhododendrons led to the front entrance, but Sally headed toward a door on the side of the house.

Katie glanced around nervously. "Gosh, this is a very fancy

house. Is your grandma nice?" she asked, her voice shaking.

"Oh yeah," said Sally. "She's super nice. Well, to me, anyway. She's only mean to people she doesn't like. Like salespeople and missionaries. She chases them. Once she chased this missionary all the way down the driveway. She was hitting him on the head with a broom. She said she wanted to hit him on the head with a shovel, but then she'd have to hide the body. Bodies are hard to hide. They turn into zombies and start showing up every day for breakfast. And my grandma *hates* having guests for breakfast. She always has her breakfast in bed. A piece of toast with two poached eggs and her special coffee. I tasted her special coffee once. It made me hiccup. My Dad took it away and said I was too young for special coffee."

Katie started to whimper quietly. "What if she doesn't like *me?*"

Sally patted her on the shoulder. "Don't worry, Katie. I promise she'll like you. It's just salespeople, missionaries, and Mean Darlene Trockworthy she doesn't like. Grandma says Darlene is on the make. That means she wears too much makeup. Which is *sooo* true. Once I saw a huge piece of her face fall off. It just peeled off like a big piece of paint peeling off a wall. It was *so* gross."

Katie turned a bit green around the gills. She took an embroidered handkerchief out of the pocket of her kilt and coughed into it. Sally went up to the side of the house and stood on tiptoe to peer in a window. Robbie was inside the house. All that could be seen of him was his rear-end, which was hanging over the edge of a large pot full of daisies. Sally pushed open the side door.

"C'mon, Katie," said Sally. "It'll be fine, you'll see."

Sally skipped into the room and grabbed hold of Robbie's shorts, hauling him out of the flowerpot. Robbie was wearing a little sailor suit and tennis shoes. A goatee of dirt circled his mouth. Sally sighed and shook her head. Robbie grinned at her and held up a worm in his chubby little fist. Sally grabbed it a split second before he put it in his mouth. She deposited the worm back into the flowerpot.

"Katie, can I borrow your handkerchief?"

Katie looked at her, then down at Robbie. She reluctantly pulled out her lacy handkerchief and handed it over. Sally scrubbed Robbie's face with it until his face turned red and the handkerchief turned brown. Robbie giggled and ran off, pulling another worm out of the pocket of his sailor suit.

"C'mon," said Sally. "Just follow Robbie. He's probably headed straight for grandma. She always stuffs him with sugar cookies. They're his favorite. After dirt, of course. And dust bunnies. He's been on a dust bunny binge lately. Yesterday my Dad found him under his bed, rolling the dust bunnies into little pancakes and pouring maple syrup on them."

Sally and Katie ran after Robbie, who led them down a hallway lined with beautiful silk wallpaper. Robbie ran his hand along the wallpaper, leaving a long brown streak of dirt. At the end of the hall he darted out of a sliding glass door.

When Sally and Katie followed Robbie through the door they found themselves on a patio which had a spectacular view of San Francisco bay and the Golden Gate Bridge.

Bill Hesslop, dressed in a suit and tie, was perched on the edge of a deckchair. Next to him, stretched out comfortably on a matching chair, was Sally's grandmother. Mrs. Belinda Worthington was a trim, stylish woman of sixty-five with white hair and blue eyes. She wore tailored trousers and a cashmere sweater. Robbie ran up to her, pulling something out of the pocket of his sailor suit.

Mrs. Worthington held out her hand. "What have you got there, Mr. Robert?"

Robbie deposited a large pink earthworm into her hand. Bill Hesslop winced, but Mrs. Worthington didn't even blink. "Well. This is a fine big wriggler, isn't he? It's too bad your grandpa isn't with us anymore. He'd take this fine specimen down to the pond and show you how to catch a fish with him. The gardener stocks the pond with trout, you know."

Robbie nodded at her solemnly. "Fishes eat worms." Robbie took the worm back and tried to put it in his mouth, but his grandmother was too quick for him. She calmly snatched up the worm and handed it to Bill Hesslop. "Bill, dear. Dispose of this, would you."

"Yes, ma'am." He sighed and carried the worm down to the lawn. Sally ran up to Mrs. Worthington and gave her a hug. "Hi, grandma! Look who I brought! This is my best friend, Katie Greenwald. Just so you know, Katie's not a salesperson or a missionary. She's a fifth-grader. We're in the same class at school."

Sally waved at Katie to come nearer, but Katie shook her head vigorously, looking terrified.

Mrs. Worthington smiled at her. She picked up a plate of cookies from a small table next to her deckchair. "Katie, I can tell by your tasteful outfit that you are a young lady of distinction. Now, I have here some wonderfully refined Petit Fours which I'm sure will appeal to your palate. Come try one."

Katie shyly approached and took a cookie. "It's very nice, ma'am."

"Such lovely manners," said Mrs. Worthington. "You could learn a thing or two from your friend, Miss Sally."

Sally tried to swallow the cookie she'd grabbed and stuffed into her mouth. "I have super good manners," she said, her voice muffled by cookie. "You told me so last time I was here, grandma. You said my compartments were spotless."

"Your comportment, dear. Your comportment was spotless. It means you were behaving like a little lady during that visit. Quite out of character, it was. You must have been ill. Perhaps a touch of flu. Usually you dash about like a little wombat that's gotten into my diet pills."

"What's a wombat?" asked Sally, taking another cookie.

"A small creature, dear. Very hyperactive. Speaking of small creatures, where is that animal you're always carting around? I hope he isn't loose in the house. Last time you were here Cook found him in the pantry. He popped out at her from behind a jar of pickled beets. She came running to me, screaming something about mice and threatening to quit. It took a bottle of my best brandy to calm her down."

"Melvin's right here, grandma. See?" Sally pointed at her shoulder, but Melvin wasn't there. Sally lifted her hair and felt around the back of her neck. No Melvin.

Her grandmother gave her a suspicious look. "Sally Jane Hesslop. Is that miniature marauder loose in my house again?"

"No, no," said Sally hurriedly. "Everything's fine, grandma. I put Melvin in a safe place, where he wouldn't bother anybody. I'll just go check on him." She made shooing motions at Katie, who backed nervously towards the house. Sally walked nonchalantly to the door, then yanked it open and pushed Katie through.

"Dang that Melvin," Sally grouched as she dashed down the hall. "He must have jumped ship and gone exploring. C'mon, Katie. We have to find him before Mrs. Beatty does. That's grandma's cook. She makes the best fudge brownies in the world, and grandma's always saying she loves Mrs. Beatty's cooking better than she loves her own family. Grandma'll be really mad if Mrs. Beatty leaves on account of Melvin."

Katie puffed along behind Sally. "Why does Mrs. Beatty hate

Melvin?" she asked breathlessly. "He's a nice hamster. Even my Mom likes him. Remember that time you brought him over to our apartment? My Mom said he was a prince among gerbils."

"Well, of course he's a prince among gerbils," said Sally. "Hamsters are way, way better than stinky old gerbils. Mrs. Beatty's problem is she can't tell that Melvin's a hamster. She thinks he's a mouse. Every time she sees him she tries to hit him with her rolling pin."

Katie gasped in horror.

Sally sang a tune as she ran:

"Mel, I know you're in the house.

Mrs. Beatty thinks you're a mouse.

Come out before you get bashed.

Hamsters look better un-smashed."

Suddenly a loud scream echoed through the house. "Shoot!" said Sally. "That's Mrs. Beatty. C'mon!"

They rushed into the kitchen, where Mrs. Beatty was standing near the oven wearing her usual uniform of flower-print dress, hairnet, and apron. Interrupted in the middle of her daily baking, she was eyeing a mixing bowl and waving a rolling pin at it. She took a step towards the bowl as it rattled. Whiskers poked over the edge, then slid back down. When they appeared again, the flour-covered head of Melvin could be seen peering over the edge of the bowl.

Melvin squirmed and wriggled and managed to pull himself up onto the rim of the bowl. It tottered and tipped over, spilling Melvin and a cascade of flour onto the kitchen counter.

Mrs. Beatty let out a war whoop and brought the rolling pin crashing down onto the counter. She missed Melvin by a whisker. He scrambled along the flour-dusted countertop, dashed around a carton of eggs, and dove head first into the open maw of a food processor. Mrs. Beatty yelled in triumph and leapt forward. She hit the 'On' switch of the food processor.

The processor began to spin, taking Melvin with it. He went around, faster and faster. Just as he was in danger of becoming hamster McNuggets he was flung out of the food processor. He flew through the air and landed face first in a bowl full of walnuts, scattering nuts everywhere.

The walnuts shifted under his feet as Melvin frantically sped up, trying to scramble out of the bowl. Nuts started flying through the air like tiny cannonballs, pelting Mrs. Beatty in the face. She raised her rolling pin and warded them off like a Jedi master blocking bullets with his light saber.

Mrs. Beatty hit a walnut through the open kitchen window, clobbering a pigeon which was flying across the lawn. It squawked and crash-landed on the grass. Ducking walnuts, Sally grabbed Melvin and jumped back out of range of Mrs. Beatty's rolling pin. Melvin shook himself, showering Sally in flour. "Jeez, Mel," said Sally. "What a mess. You need a bath. You look like a dumpling with feet."

"A bath!" yelled Mrs. Beatty, shaking her rolling pin. "Do not talk to me of baths! What is needed is a mousetrap with a nice strong spring. Snap!" She whacked her rolling pin down on the counter with a bang.

Sally and Katie jumped. "C'mon, Mrs. Beatty," said Sally. "You don't really mean that. Melvin's very sorry he disturbed your cooking. Aren't you, Mel?" Sally held Melvin up to her eyes and glared at him.

Melvin stared back at her and yawned. He was clearly not in an apologetic mood, rolling pin or no rolling pin.

Mrs. Beatty snorted and shook the rolling pin at them. "Out of my kitchen! All of you! I am making croque en bouche. It is a very delicate process, not to be interrupted by small children and mice! Out!"

Sally, Katie, and Melvin beat a hasty retreat.

"I BET THEY'VE gone down to the stables," said Sally, surveying the empty patio. Her father, grandmother, and Robbie were nowhere to be seen. A lone sparrow pecked at the crumbs of the Petit Fours. "C'mon, maybe grandma'll let us ride Max!" She dashed down the steps of the patio two at a time and headed across the lawn.

"Who's Max?" Katie asked, breath coming in gasps as she tried to keep up.

"He's a Shetland pony," said Sally, slowing down so Katie could catch up. "He's super gentle. You can ride on his back without a saddle. Plus he's got long blond hair called a mane. Grandma lets me brush it. When it's brushed Max looks just like a princess. Well, he would if he weren't a horse. Or a boy."

"I don't know if I want to meet Max," Katie said dubiously. "I think I might be afraid of horses."

"What do you mean, 'might' be? Don't you know?"

"I'm not sure," said Katie. "I've never seen a horse, not in person I mean."

Sally changed course and headed for a birdbath in the center of the lawn. "You have *so* seen a horse. Remember that policeman who yelled at us just cause we were climbing that lamppost? He was riding a horse."

"He was yelling at *you*, not me," said Katie. "*I* wasn't climbing the lamppost. I was holding your backpack and Melvin. Melvin didn't want to climb the lamppost either. And the horse was way over across the street. If the horse had been on our side of the street I'm pretty sure I would have been afraid of it."

"Well, you won't be afraid of Max. And anyway, he's a pony, not a horse. Ponies are kinda like horses that have shrunk. You know, like that time my Dad wasn't home and I did the laundry all by myself and all of my Dad's sweaters shrank. It was weird. They came out of the dryer looking like little kids clothes. Robbie wears them now. Your Mom's got some nice sweaters. I specially like that pink fuzzy one. If you ever want some new clothes, just do the laundry." Sally stopped at the birdbath. It had moss growing along its sides and was full of rainwater. A sparrow was perched on the rim, watching them warily. "Okay, Mel. It's bath time."

She lowered Melvin into the water. When she let go he promptly sank down to the moldy bottom of the birdbath. Sally grabbed him off the bottom and swished him around in the water, leaving a trail of flour floating like dust on the water's surface.

"There you go, Mel. Much better. Though I can see you're overdue for your Secret Agent swimming lessons. You might want to sign up next time you're in Washington BC. And make sure you use Water Wings the first time. Katie uses them."

"Oh, yes", said Katie, nodding enthusiastically. "Definitely use Water Wings, Melvin. One time, Charlie Sanderson pushed me into the pool at Rimrock Park when I wasn't wearing my Water Wings. The lifeguard had to pull me out and hit my back to get all the water out. I had pool water in my tummy for days afterward. You could hear it splashing around when I walked."

Melvin regarded her with appropriate solemnity upon hearing this information.

Sally pulled off Melvin's wet sweater and set him on her shoulder. "I hope he doesn't catch cold. Melvin's very delicate. And sensitive. My Dad says he's an old soul. That means he's a good listener. He knows all kinds of super-secret stuff, but he never tells anyone. That would be against the Super Secret Hamster Code of Rules and Regulations. Nope, if you've got a secret, tell a hamster."

"Gerbils are verbal

And sip tea that is herbal.

They gossip and chat

About this and that.

So if you've got secrets to tell,

A hamster is swell.

Do what you will,

They'll never spill."

Sally and Katie (and Melvin, shivering on Sally's shoulder and dripping water down the back of her t-shirt) followed a stone-covered path which led from the lawn into a grove of birch trees. A patch of bluebells clustered under the waving trees. Sally picked one of the tiny flowers and held it up for Melvin to sniff. He nosed it warily and then suddenly swallowed it, causing hamster convulsions as he choked on the petals. To prevent himself from falling off Sally's shoulder Melvin dug his claws into her T-shirt.

"Ouch! Dang it Melvin, that hurt." Sally detached him from her T-shirt and held him up at eye level. "What do you say? Hmm?"

Melvin was not known for his expressiveness, but it did appear that his whiskers had a hint of apology about them.

"That's right," said Sally. "You say you're sorry. Grandma's always saying how I need some etiquette lessons. Maybe you should have some too. You can't be a Secret Agent if you don't have good etiquette."

"What's etiquette?" asked Katie.

"It's these rules on how to behave in all situations. Like, if you burp really loudly at a fancy dinner party you should point to the person next to you. Hamsters know all these rules automatically, but I think maybe Melvin needs a refresher course."

Up ahead the trees thinned out and the path they were on ended at a white-fenced corral. Mrs. Worthington was mounted on a chestnut mare, putting the glossy-coated horse through its paces. Together horse and rider turned and spun expertly around the corral. Mrs. Worthington sat with her back straight as a ruler. They picked up speed and sailed over a jump made of red and white striped poles, the horse's hooves clearing the top pole with ease. Bill Hesslop and Robbie clapped from their seats on a pile of hay bales.

"Wow! Look at your grandmother!" said Katie as they climbed onto the fence of the corral to watch. "How come she doesn't fall off?"

"Oh, she practices all the time." said Sally. "Grandma says she started riding when she was two. Her Dad put her on a pony and then gave it a spanking. It took off and ran right through some rose bushes and then up those steps in the backyard and into the house. My Dad says grandma is exaggerating about the 'into the house' part. He says I get my linguistic flexibility from her. That means I can roll my tongue into funny shapes." Sally stuck her tongue out at Katie and rolled it into a "U" shape.

Katie looked impressed and tried to roll her tongue too, but couldn't quite manage it. She pushed at it with her fingers, but finally gave up. "Your grandmother must be very rich, to live in this big house and have horses and everything. How come you and your Dad and Robbie live in such a small apartment?"

"It's because of the prostate," said Sally, laying Melvin's wet sweater on the top rail of the fence to dry. "My Mom died without a will, so the estate went into Prostate. When it came out all the money stayed with my grandma, cause she's my Mom's mom. Also my Mom and Dad weren't married. They were free spirits. That means they saved lots of money by not getting married. My Dad says that weddings are just huge holes people throw cash into. Which is just stupid. If I had lots of money I wouldn't throw it down a hole. I'd vest it in the sock market. That's what grandma does. My Dad says she's rolling in money. That means she spreads money on the floor and does somersaults on it."

Katie nodded, looking impressed.

Sally waved at her grandmother, who wheeled her horse and trotted over to them.

"Hello, Miss Sally. Would you like to ride Violet here? I've given her a thorough workout, so she's nice and calm."

Bill Hesslop jumped off his hay bale and hurried up to the fence, looking rather alarmed. "I don't think that's such a good idea. Sally, why don't you ride that little pony you were on last time? He's more your speed. He's right over there."

Bill Hesslop pointed to Max, a chubby little Shetland pony who was munching grass in a pasture next to the corral.

"Nonsense, Bill dear," said Mrs. Worthington. "Why, I started riding full-grown horses when I was five. She'll be fine. We'll start slow. Sally dear, come sit up here in front of me."

Mrs. Worthington guided her horse up next to the fence. Sally handed Melvin to Katie and climbed onto the top bar of the fence. Her grandmother wrapped one arm around Sally's waist and hoisted her into the saddle in front of her. They trotted slowly around the corral, Sally whooping with delight and Bill Hesslop watching nervously. Katie climbed down from the fence and made herself comfortable on a hay bale. She put Melvin on her lap and gave him a good scratch behind the ears. Both of them looked extremely glad they were sitting on a hay bale and not on a horse.

Robbie sat next to them for a while, swinging his chubby legs and chewing on a handful of grass he had yanked up from the pony's pasture, but soon he started to fidget. He climbed down from his hay bale and toddled off toward Max with a determined gleam in his eye. Katie eyed him worriedly, but decided that if she had to choose between watching Melvin and watching Robbie, Melvin was definitely the easier choice.

Max had tired of grass and was ambling over to a pile of sacks bulging with grain which someone had unwisely left in his pasture. With his strong front teeth he tore a hole in one corner of the top sack and a tiny waterfall of grain poured out. As Max indulged himself in this unexpected snack Robbie quietly pulled himself up onto the wobbling pile of grain sacks. He balanced precariously, like a diver on a diving board, then reached out with both hands and awkwardly slid himself stomach first onto the pony's back, where he lay like a very lumpy saddle. Max pulled his nose out of the grain pile in surprise and twisted his head around. He eyed Robbie's rear end curiously, giving a little shake to see if the strange object would fall off. Robbie giggled. Max pricked up his ears at this, deciding this might be a fun game. He started at a slow trot across the pasture. Robbie bounced up and down, laughing hysterically.

Max circled his pasture a few times then headed for the gate, which was closed but not locked. He gave the bars a push with his nose and they were off toward the estate's long gravel drive and freedom.

Behind them footsteps pounded on the gravel. Max sped up, his round belly swaying from side to side. Robbie's giggles got even louder. It looked like the two adventurers were going to pull off their escape into the wide world. But, alas, reality (and a puffing parent) prevailed.

Bill Hesslop ran forward and grabbed Robbie off the pony's back. "That's enough, you two," he said, gasping for air. He set Robbie on his feet and shook his finger at Max. "Max, you should know better. And you, Robbie. With all the dirt and cookies you've managed to tuck away today, all that bouncing is going to make you spew like Old Faithful."

Mrs. Worthington and Sally rode up on Violet. The chestnut mare nickered in a disapproving manner at the pony. Max shook his blond mane at her and began to calmly munch a cluster of dandelions at his feet.

"Oh, I wouldn't worry about our Mr. Robert's digestion," said Mrs. Worthington. "He has a stomach like cast iron. He gets it from his grandpa. That man could eat a five-course Sunday dinner, top if off with three desserts, and then go on the WhirlyGig ride at the State Fair carnival without so much as a twinge of heartburn. Though, I admit he didn't share little Mr. Robert's fondness for soil sampling. You really ought to cure the child of that, Bill dear. I caught him snacking on the compost under my roses the last time he was here. It's a good thing I tell my gardener not to use pesticides."

Bill Hesslop sighed. "Yes, ma'am. I've tried to get Robbie to stop eating dirt. Our doctor says it's just a phase he's going through. He's like a puppy. He'll eat anything. Next he'll probably start chewing on shoes. Well, it's been a pleasure, as always, but we need to get going. I need to get Sally to her school. Her play is tonight and they have one last rehearsal."

"You're coming, right grandma?" said Sally as she slid off of Violet's back. "It's gonna be super terrific. It's about the Pilgrims and the first Thanksgiving. I'm a Squall."

"You mean a Squaw, Sally." said her father.

Sally nodded. "Right. If you're a Naïve American and a girl, then you're a Squall. The boys are Braves, like the baseball team.

All the Brownies from my troop are in the play. Course, we don't have boys in the Brownies, so there are some Cub Scouts in the play, but it's still gonna be good."

Mrs. Worthington dismounted. "I'm sure even the Cub Scouts will be unable to dim your thespian brilliance my dear. Of course I'll be there. It will be the highlight of my social season."

End of Excerpt